MINDERS

MARK FASSETT

MINDERS

Mark Fassett

Ravenstar Press
Monroe, WA

Published 2014 by Ravenstar Press
Monroe, WA
http://www.ravenstarpress.com

Designed by Mark Fassett
http://www.markfassett.com

Cover Design by Mark Fassett
Images used:
Background © Rolffimages | Dreamstime.com

ISBN: 978-0692210987

Acknowledgements

I'd like to thank everyone that has helped me in getting this book ready. My friends Rebecca M. Senese, David Michael, Kendra Harrington, and Michael Canfield did me a great service in reading it and telling me what's what. My wife stuck with me throughout, and my kids were special lights in this universe, even when things weren't going so well.

I'd also like to thank Kristine Kathryn Rusch and Dean Wesley Smith for creating a community of writers through their workshops that is so supporting and understanding. This book is for them, as much as it is for anyone.

CHAPTER 1

The smell wafting low along the tiny river at the bottom of the sewer is something I have not smelled before—sweet, almost like a berry, but it stings my nose at the same time.

I sit up and my feet splash into the water running past me. It's cold, but it doesn't bother me. Cold never does.

With my head up, the smell fades a bit—still there, but not as strong. The scent is heavy, it seems.

I test the breeze in the tunnel with a wet finger. It's not stagnant. I can feel it move past my finger from upstream.

I dip my nose back into the flow of the scent and it strengthens. It smells like food, and my stomach rumbles. I haven't eaten in a few days. I don't need to eat every day, or even more than once a week, but food is always welcome. I must discover the source and see if it truly is food.

I get to my feet and walk up stream, staying clear of the water as much as possible in an effort to keep quiet until I reach the next junction in the sewer. The passage I'm in continues on, another passage leads off to my right.

I duck my head, put my nose into the flow of that scent one more time, and it's still there, slightly stronger. I am pleased I wasn't wrong about the direction.

I check each of the possible passages. The scent is stronger in the passage ahead of me, so I continue my journey in that direction.

I follow the scent past several more junctions and it continues to grow stronger—now strong enough that I no longer have to dip my head to follow it, strong enough that dipping my head makes it almost overpowering. My stomach churns and churns. It's as if the scent is causing me to hunger.

The tunnel ahead bends sharply to the left. A soft glow illuminates the bend, but the glow doesn't hurt my eyes. I suspect the light comes from a light bulb. It concerns me for a moment, as I can't recall any lights in this tunnel, but the allure of the overpowering scent is more than enough to override those concerns.

I approach the bend, eager to see around the corner.

A hand shoots out from the shadows and takes me by the arm, halting my progress.

I spin in its grasp, but the hand is strong. It doesn't let go.

"They hunt, brother," says a voice I do not recognize.

A large man steps out from the shadows, and for the first time, I can smell the putrid stench of him, but in the presence of that other sweet scent, I can tolerate his odor. He stands taller than me by a foot, at least. His head nearly scrapes the top of the sewer. The glow is not bright enough to show me all the features of his face, but I get the impression of kind eyes and pock-marked skin. He's not attacking me.

That realization, and his stench, breaks the spell of the sweet scent, allowing his words to reach my brain.

"Who hunts?" I ask.

"Division six," he says. "Run back the way you came. Leave these sewers and find another place to hide."

"Why? What is Division Six?" I ask, confused.

"It doesn't matter. They hunt us, and those they take never come back."

He pushes me back down the tunnel from whence I came.

"Run," he says. "Find a new home."

He uses his great size to block the source of the scent from me. I could not pass him were I to try. Whatever I am, whatever caused me to be the thing I have become, it did not give me any extra strength.

But I stand, looking at him, hoping he will move. The allure of the sweet scent and the hunger in my belly is that strong.

"Run!" he shouts.

And then, in the background, I hear the voices of men.

The pfft pfft of dart guns follow.

The giant flinches.

His hand slips a little.

Another pfft, and the giant flinches again.

My fear finally overcomes my hunger.

I turn and run.

CHAPTER 2

I like starlight. You might think that it would hurt just as much as sunlight, since stars are, after all, really far away suns. A friend once suggested that the atmosphere filters out whatever is left of the ultra-violet light, or whatever it is that causes me pain. I can look at the stars, and even the moon, without discomfort.

Unfortunately, on the city streets of Seattle, I can't see starlight. All I see are the neon lights and streetlights and billboard lights. It gets worse every year, it seems.

Those lights bathe me in their glow as I crawl out of the sewer several blocks away from where Division Six, or whatever the giant had called them, were trying to lure me. I still puzzle over why he put himself between me and them. Any rational being would not have done it for a stranger. I would not have done it for him.

Yet the act was done and I stand in the street, scared and confused. They shot him with dart guns. They weren't trying to kill him, or me. Why do they want me?

Even this late at night, a few people walk the sidewalks around me, and they are staring while simultaneously trying to pretend like they're not looking. The neon lights are not my friends, and there are no dark places to hide. Even if I could find a place close by, I cannot help but continually glance back at the entrance to the sewer in fear that the men with the guns will come boiling out to catch me.

It's clear to me that I have to move to another place, which is easy enough, but I wonder if they know of those places, too. Will they search the train tunnels and under the freeways? Are they hunting me specifically, or are they just hunting those of my kind? Why are they hunting in the first place?

I know I need to visit one of my friends, but I fear to do so. I don't want to bring them any trouble, but I need answers, and the public libraries close at nine—hours past, judging by the very few vehicles passing by on the street. I wouldn't be able to access them even if I wanted to, not until later in the year when darkness fell a little earlier. Summer has become my least favorite season.

I ponder my options. Mary is closest to where I am, and she always keeps a fresh set of clothes for me. I don't like going there, though. She was my girlfriend at the time of my change, and I love her. She moved on, had a husband, kids with him. He died too early of lung cancer some fifteen years ago. I had always kept an eye on her and screwed up my courage to visit and console her when he died, but it was hard then. She had changed, grown older, nearing forty years old while I still looked like I was twenty-two. She had apologized for giving up on me and leaving. I told her I was sorry her husband died and to not worry about me, that I was fine, even though my heart hurt inside. I knew then it could never be the same, but I did look in on her from time to time, and she made me look respectable from time to time.

But she would not know anything about how to deal with Division Six.

George, on the other hand, he might. Ex-military and a recently retired police officer, he would have the resources and perhaps the knowledge to find out something about Division Six. But he lives across town. Too far to walk before the sun comes up. I'd have to take a cab or a bus.

My third and final possibility is Joe. He is a scientist of sorts, mad scientist, more likely. A biology professor at the college I was attending when the change came over me. I didn't see him for a long time until our paths crossed at a park just after dusk. Since then, he has spent many of the intervening years trying to find an answer to my condition, or at least a way to let me come out in sunlight without pain, to no avail. My body has resisted everything he has tried.

He isn't much farther away than Mary, and he has the computer setup that will make things easier—untraceable, he says. That's what I need right now. If there is anything about Division Six on the internet, Joe can find it. If that doesn't work out, I can trek across town tomorrow night.

CHAPTER 3

Joe's house sits in a neighborhood of single family residences just west of the downtown core. The homes were built, I think, in the early fifties. They're all small by today's standards, and it's obvious they all started with the same basic layout. Square with a front porch. Not attractive at all, and if you are a mad scientist, not a bad place to hang out, usually.

I keep to the shadows as much as I can, dancing between the cones of light the streetlights put out. If I were normal, it might make one suspicious, but one of the bonuses of my condition is that I am somehow near invisible in the dark. People just do not see me, despite my near white skin. I don't even have to wear black—they just look right past.

But in the light, Joe (and Mary and George and others) has confirmed, I almost glow. It is near impossible to *not* see me.

So I keep to the dark spaces as much as possible.

In this way, I walk the fifteen blocks to Joe's neighborhood.

With only one block to go, I notice that the dark of night has started to lift. I have an hour, at most, before I must be hidden from the sun. It's only one block, but I pick up my pace, nonetheless. I do not want to be caught out in the sun.

In my haste, I stop paying attention to the pools of light. Few are awake at this hour, and even fewer are outside.

Ahead of me, there is a hedge, eight feet high, at least, that blocks the view of Joe's street. The owner of the hedge has kept the sides trimmed, but I do not think they've ever topped it.

I am about a foot from the corner when I notice the first black car, a non-descript sedan that could have been made by any of the Detroit auto-makers. It wouldn't normally have set off any alarm bells in me, but with the events in the sewer, I still feel on edge. The car looks too clean for a car on Joe's street.

I pull up and stare at the car. I am in a shadow, by luck more than anything, and the car is in shadow, too. But light from a streetlamp glares off the car window. I cannot see into it to see if there is anyone inside. Maybe they are already aware that I am here.

I look up at the sky. It's growing lighter, and I am running out of time. I cannot stand here forever, and I am too far away from any of my normal hiding spots.

I wait a couple minutes, watching the car.

It does not move.

I risk stepping around the corner. The car still does not move.

Either they can't see me, or they are not in the car, or the car is...

No. There are three other similarly non-descript black vehicles on the street.

Joe has been compromised.

I kneel down in the shadow and try to make myself as small as possible while I think.

If I were still human, I know my heart would be thumping away in my chest, but my heart doesn't change its rhythm to help me adapt to stress anymore. It beats the same staid rhythm it always does, as if it's on autopilot.

I glance up at the sky. No more than fifty minutes until I must be out of sight, now. The only place I know within reach is Joe's house. But I can't go to Joe's house, not with Division Six all over it.

I should leave, find an unboarded front or back porch to hide under for the day.

But if I do that, what happens to Joe? Can I just leave him with Division Six? What are they doing to him?

Another darker thought breaks through my concern about Joe.

Did he tell them about me? Did he tell them how to find me?

No. Joe would not have told them where to find me. He could not have known where I would be right at that moment. I cannot believe he would give me up without a fight. He fought them. I am sure of it.

A plan forms in my mind. It is not a smart plan, but it is a necessary one. I need Joe, and as certain I am that he fought for me, I know right this moment he needs me.

I am not a vampire. I do not suck blood in order to live. I do not have superhuman speed or strength.

I am not a vampire.

I am worse.

CHAPTER 4

Staying to the quickly fading shadows, I sneak across the street to come up behind the first of the Division Six cars.

I have forty-five minutes to do this, and my advantage fades with every minute that passes. I must be quick.

I peer inside the car. It's empty of people, but I can see the radio, the GPS, the dash-mounted laptop, all obviously government issue. This is not the car of one of the homeowners.

I back away quickly, up against a low chain-link fence—no more than three feet high—the kind of fence that keeps little kids and little dogs in the yard, but no one else. I don't need the Division Six men to see me against their car.

I flit from shadow to shadow, hiding behind shrubs and bushes where I can, moving up the street toward the next shiny black government sedan. At each quick stop, I glance around, looking for the lookouts. I know they're there. They must be. But I haven't seen one yet, and I am no more than ten feet from the car.

Carefully, I approach the car and look inside while trying to keep one eye watching for the men I know should be there.

This car, too, is empty.

A shred of worry starts to eat at me, but there is little I can do. They are all in, or around, Joe's house. It would be better if they were spread out so that I could take them one at a time. It would be better if I knew how many had arrived with each car.

I move on to the next vehicle, conscious of the ever brightening sky. My skin will soon begin to tingle, the warning that I have little time to find shelter.

The next car is actually an SUV. Big, black, and right out of every spy movie ever made. The rear and side windows are tinted. I cannot see in through them. I wonder if someone inside is already watching me, but the vehicle remains still. They have not seen me, or there is no one there, or they do not recognize I am who they seek.

I move up the side of the vehicle, toward the front, until I can see through the front window. This vehicle, too, is empty.

For a moment, I entertain the idea of testing the door handles to see if they open. The protection the tinted windows would give me might be enough to allow me to find a parking garage to hide in.

But it was probably one of those new models that had a chip in the key that was required to be present to start, assuming an alarm didn't go off. I'll never be able to jack it. I decide to jettison the idea before I even attempt to open the doors.

The last of the Division Six cars stands beyond Joe's driveway. Checking it would take extra time, and I would have to double back.

I glance up at the sky. To the east, it has started to lighten to the point that I can almost see the blue. Either the world is turning faster, or I am taking too much time.

I dash toward the yard of Joe's neighbor. Joe's yard has only a huge expanse of a lawn with a six foot fence along the rear property line. The lawn covers every inch of his property that is not paved or built upon. Mowing it is the only concession he makes to keeping his yard up. There are no other plants that aren't weeds. He doesn't have time for them.

His neighbor's yard, however, is shielded by tall, thin, emerald greens. The trees guard the property line between the two homes. I slip behind them and move along the row of trees until I am about even with the front of Joe's house before I search for a hole in the branches.

I find a small hole, barely large enough to see Joe's front porch. Two men stand there, dressed in black suits, arms down at their sides, ready and watching. They look a bit like Secret Service men, ex-military. I don't know what I expected, but I should have expected this. No governmental entity would send office drones to do this kind of work, whatever kind of work it is. Two out front means at least two inside.

I decide to check the back. Perhaps I can slip in through the back door, or if that fails, into or under someone's garden shed.

Joe's neighbor has an old wooden fence that bars me from his backyard unless I want to jump it. I don't. I would only have to jump it again to get into Joe's yard.

I walk up to the fence, though, and slip between it and the last of the emerald greens, and then dash across the eight feet of lawn to come up against the side of Joe's house.

The siding of the house is covered in a slimy moss, a present from the shade of his neighbor's trees. I make a note to tell Joe he needs to pressure wash it. He forgets these things.

As quietly as I can, greatly aided by the soft grass, I make my way to the back of the house.

I reach the corner and peer around it.

Unexpectedly, there is no one out back. The house has two back doors. A traditional door that leads into the garage, and a sliding glass door from a slightly raised deck that leads into the kitchen. I would prefer to enter the kitchen first, but I fear the noise of the sliding door would bring Division Six men running.

I feel the first tingle, the final warning that I need to find shelter from the sun. I have minutes, at most, before the tingling becomes burning.

The door at the back of the garage is closer.

I work my way to it, keeping low and up against the back of Joe's house. There are no windows on the back wall of the garage, but it is bad enough that I'm creeping around out back while there are Division Six men in the house. I don't need Joe's neighbors calling the police—not that most of them would, but you never know.

When I get to the door, I bend at the knees and reach my hand down to the left of it, to a spot where the siding and the foundation meet. Joe keeps his key there, in a little space right behind the bottom layer of the siding. He told me about it once, so that I could enter if I needed shelter like I do now. I don't think he ever expected me to use it when he was home.

I fumble around for the key, touch something metal, then the key falls into my palm.

I can feel the sun on the back of my neck where my hat doesn't quite meet the collar of my coat. I tilt my head back a little, but I know it's only a temporary solution. I need inside.

The door unlocks with a quiet click and then opens without squealing.

The garage is wonderfully dark and I slip inside and shut the door behind me, blocking out the rising sun and its torturous rays. I am safe, momentarily.

CHAPTER 5

Once my eyes adjust—it does not take long—I work my way around the accumulated junk that fills Joe's garage. I want to get to the door that leads to the main part of his house so that I can listen and determine what my next move might be.

There aren't any car parts or other typical things you would find in a normal person's garage. Instead, Joe has a laundry list of odd scientific equipment from the last thirty years that he just can't stand to give away. Some of it is in pieces, parts scavenged for other equipment that is still in use, and some of it looks fully functional, but older than I am.

Movement through the mess is tedious, the paths between the equipment miniscule. I do not want to upset even one piece for fear of bringing Division Six into the garage. My assumption is that they have already been in here and determined that most of this is useless crap.

When I reach the door, relieved that I have avoided toppling anything over, I place my ear against it and listen.

For the first few moments, I hear nothing.

But then I hear a voice, rough and angry. "Where else could he be?"

"How should I know?" Joe asks. His voice does not sound scared. It sounds just as angry as the Division Six voice.

"You've worked with him for twenty years. I would think you would know where else he might be."

"He could be anywhere. He wanders around. I told you the one place I know where he spends time. Beyond that, I haven't got any idea."

"Joe," says a female voice, kinder and gentler than the first voice, but still full of steel, "I know how close you were to him. He's not safe out there. Not anymore. Just tell us where."

I wait for Joe's answer while I struggle to make sense of the subtext. Joe told them where to find me. Is Joe working for them? How does she know how close we are, or is she just trying to soothe Joe?

"Like I said, I haven't got a clue. He always came here. The only reason I knew about the sewer was that he talked about it once."

"There must be other places he talked about," says the woman.

"If he had told me, you would know. You've read all my journals. I want him found as much as you do."

"You aren't hiding anything from us?"

The sharp report of a hand slamming against the Formica kitchen counter-top reaches my ears as Joe begins to yell. "God dammit! It's your own damn fault you brought Taggart in on this. How did you let him get in between you and Steve? How did your men let him off the leash?"

I want to leave. The betrayal runs deep. Joe hadn't just told Division Six who I was and where to find me. Joe had told them, let them read, everything he knew about me.

But I can't leave. I can't go outside, not now. There is nowhere to run to. I have to hope they don't find me here in Joe's garage.

My anger is rising, I can feel it. My heart doesn't beat any faster, but after thinking Joe was my friend for all these years, I find out he's been telling people about me. No. Not people. The government. Division Six, whoever they are.

"We had nothing to do with Taggart," says the woman. "You know that. It wasn't our call."

"Nothing is ever your call," says Joe. I can hear the bitterness in him. I wonder what he will do if he discovers I am listening to his conversation.

"Do you think he will come here?" asks the woman.

"If you all didn't scare him off, he would be here already." Joe sounds defeated. I wonder why. "I'm going upstairs to get some sleep. You're welcome to stay, but I've got nothing else for you."

"I'll stay," says the woman. Then she switches to a much harder voice, one familiar with command. "Take the others and get your rest. Be back by sundown."

"You're staying?" says the voice that had remained quiet while she questioned Joe.

"Yes."

"But..."

"The subject is not here, and there's little danger until sundown, and I have some reading to do." She knows I'm dangerous, I can tell.

"Yessir."

I hear feet start to tramp through the house, footsteps receding as the Division Six men left.

I stay at the door for a few minutes longer, hoping to hear anything else that might enlighten me as to why they are after me, why Joe is working with them, but the wait is fruitless. They have all left.

I head back into the junk-pile of the garage and search for a place to lie down, another long day of waiting for the sun to go down ahead of me.

CHAPTER 6

I open my eyes. The garage is dark, like before, but darker now. The line of light that had earlier seeped from under the garage door to provide a dim light turned dark while I slept.

I curse myself. I had hoped to wake before the sun disappeared for the night, before the Division Six men returned. I had hoped to talk with Joe, though what I might have said to him was lost with my sleep.

Now, those chances are gone and there is little I can do but leave.

Still, Joe's betrayal is a sore point, and I am having a hard time accepting it. He is helping these people to find me, but at the same time, it almost sounds like he is trying to protect me.

But then, why, assuming Taggart was the brute that told me to run, would Taggart tell me to run? I have an urge to go in and find out what is really behind Joe's duplicity, but I restrain it. I can come back any time.

I push myself up from the nest I had made among the detritus of Joe's experiments.

I quickly work out a plan. I'll stop by Mary's to get a change of clothes, and maybe food, and then I'll head cross-town to George's place. I should have gone there in the first place.

"You're awake," says Joe's voice.

He is sitting not far from my hiding place, partially hidden behind a pile of junk, barricaded from me by a wall of it.

"Explain yourself," I say.

"What is there to explain?"

"I heard you earlier. Why do they want me and why are you working for them?"

I start to move through the pile of junk toward the back of the garage and the door that leads to freedom. I do not trust the situation. If Joe is in here, they know it.

"I've always worked for them," Joe says. "They won't let you go. They need you too much."

"I don't understand. Tell me why."

I can see Joe better, now. He is sitting on a small stool. He was waiting for me to wake up. I wonder how long. His face is drawn, defeated. He does not look at me, which is no surprise. It is dark in the garage. He didn't turn on the light. I suspect he did that to try to keep me comfortable.

"They haven't told me why," Joe says. "They *have* told me that you are in danger, and they need to bring you in. I swear that's all I know."

"You're lying. They know everything about me. How long have you been telling them about me?"

Joe sighs.

I know what that means.

"Don't bother answering," I say, and put my hand on the doorknob. "One last question. Are they waiting for me outside?"

Joe hesitates.

"No," he says.

He's lying.

I take my hand from the doorknob.

I work my way through the mess in the garage to where Joe is sitting. He looks up just as I arrive. I kneel down next to him.

"Why, Joe?" I whisper.

"It's my job," he says.

"How many are there?"

He hesitates again. "Five."

I reach out and place my hand on his head, almost like I'm patting a dog, but he knows what I'm doing. I can feel him shiver.

"How many?" I ask.

He doesn't hesitate this time. "Twelve. Four out back, four out front, four inside. You won't get through them all."

"They sent you in here to talk to me. Why?"

"They don't want anyone hurt, least of all you. They're trying to save you, Steve."

Right. I've had people try to save me before. It's never about saving me. There is always some other motive.

"Save me from what?" I ask.

"Someone is killing people like you," Joe says.

"I can't die," I say. I've been shot, stabbed, set on fire, even the sun doesn't kill me, it just hurts a whole lot.

"You can die if they take off your head or if they put a big enough hole through your heart."

I shiver and Joe looks up, having felt the shiver through my hand. This worries me, especially the hole in the heart part.

"How has this person killed the others?"

"Decapitation. And we don't know that it's one person. It may be several."

Several. I can imagine.

"How much longer will your *friends* wait?" I ask.

"Possibly not much longer. At some point, they will assume you killed me."

"I want to," I say. "You should have told me long ago."

Joe says nothing, but his head bows underneath my palm.

"What is their interest in me? Why did Taggart intervene?"

"Taggart. I have no idea."

"He's working for them like you are?"

Joe nods, then looks up at me. "He was. Now, I don't know."

"He told me to run, that Division Six was after me. Why would he tell me that if what you say is true?"

"I don't know."

"You don't seem to know much."

"I just do research," Joe says. "I don't know anything."

"Did you know Taggart?"

"Not before they found him."

I just don't know what to do. Who do I trust, now? Joe, who says they're protecting me and I won't be hurt, or Taggart, who works with them and told me to run? I'm not sure I can trust either one of them. And if there is someone out there trying to kill me? It sounds like a story meant to scare me into doing what they want.

I flex my fingers on Joe's head—the hairspray in his thinning hair crunches under my fingers.

"Please, Steve. I was only trying to help you."

"I thought you were my friend." My voice sounds colder to my ears than I have heard it in years.

"I am," Joe pleads.

"Friends don't sell friends out," I say. "You should have told me years ago."

I pull my hand from his head, cock my arm back, then hit him in the back of the head. He can't see it coming in the dark. He's not one of us. He falls to the ground, out cold without making a sound, which is what I want.

I am out of time. I know it.

I turn to the rear door, planning how I will try to escape, and my eyes catch on the electrical panel. I have a new plan, and the corners of my mouth involuntarily turn up.

CHAPTER 7

I don't have much time, if I have any, but I need something, anything, that might block those darts they shot at Taggart. I don't want to end up asleep in Division Six's arms.

I spy a garbage can in the corner, the old galvanized metal ones. It has a lid. Cheesy, I know, but it's what I've got to work with. When I pick it up, I feel like a kid again, for a moment, ready to slay dragons.

I find a pipe nearby, too, about three feet long. I pick it up and give it a test swing, careful not to knock any of Joe's junk over. It'll do. I don't really want to kill anyone, as I figure that will only make them more determined to catch me. Besides, absorption takes too long, and I just won't have time for it if Joe's count of four Division Six people waiting outside each door is true.

The seconds I have left are ticking away. They're going to storm the garage, soon, if Joe doesn't come out.

They will storm the garage as soon as I flip the main breaker switch.

I make my way to the power box, pop open the door, and flip the main power breaker to the house. The nearly inaudible hum that accompanies all the powered devices in a home disappears.

I leave the breaker box immediately and start making my way through the maze of discarded junk toward the back door.

The door to the house opens cautiously. I keep an eye on it, but until they get the lights on, they won't be able to see me. It's the rear door that I am worried about. I do not want them blocking my exit through that door.

The rear door cracks open.

Damn.

They're coming in.

I give up on stealth and bull my way through the piles of junk toward the door.

"Stop!" shouts the woman from earlier, but I know she can't see me very well, if at all. It's too dark in the garage.

A flashlight, two, spear out from doorway to the house.

I keep moving.

The noise of the junk falling over is loud—breaking glass, metal devices clanking to the concrete floor.

I am near the rear door.

A man clad in black body armor flings it open. He has a helmet on with a plexiglass face shield.

Good thing I picked up the pipe.

I raise it above my head and bring it down on the man's head, and he crumples to the floor.

One down.

I jump over him, and swing the pipe at another man, armored just like the first. He, too, falls without having brought his weapon to bear.

I hear the whiz of darts behind me.

I can only hope the shooters can't see me well as a third man in front of me already has his weapon up.

I bring up my trashcan lid and duck behind it as I rush forward.

Darts clang off the lid. One, two, three, four of them in rapid succession until I barrel through him, knocking him to the turf outside.

I'm out in the night air. A cloud hovers above, lucky for me.

Bright lights flash on, flooding the back yard with a painful sun-like glare. It burns the skin of my face. I try to raise my trashcan-lid shield to block it, but it comes from all sides.

I want to fall to the ground, cover myself, but I must keep moving. I can't let them catch me.

I run.

The pfft of a dart gun reaches my ears a split second before the dart bites into my shoulder.

It stings, but it's not enough to bring me down. Not yet.

One of the lights stands just off to my left, it's giant orange-yellow lamp blazing away atop it. I turn toward it, and reach out as I run by, knocking it to the ground with the pipe as I pass. The bulb in it shatters and the blazing light dims.

I can see better now, and Joe lied to me again. There were more than four of them out here. More like a dozen.

Another dart gun, another dart. This one whizzes by my ear with a rush of air.

After knocking over the light, with the back-swing of the pipe, I catch one of the men in the gut, doubling him over. He drops his weapon. My trashcan-lid shield catches a dart.

I'm having trouble lifting the shield. My shoulder is growing tired. I rush out into the dark of Joe's back yard, but flashlights follow me. More darts fly my way, but they miss to all sides.

I dash sideways, and darts fly through the space where I had just been. I hear them pass in between the shouts of the Division Six men.

I need cover while I climb the fence.

I run for Joe's storage shed, which is where he keeps his lawn equipment.

I make it around the shed to the back. There is just space enough to fit between it and the chain-link fence that separates Joe's yard from the neighboring yard behind.

I can feel whatever sort of drug they put in the dart spread throughout my shoulder and down my arm. Soon, I won't be able to use it. Already, the garbage can lid is growing too heavy to hold.

I drop it to the ground. I drop the pipe, too. No need to carry the extra weight.

I slip my toes into the gaps in the fence and climb.

The boots of the Division Six men grow closer.

"He's going over," one of them shouts as the sounds of my climb spread throughout the yard.

I'm half way up. I imagine them rounding the corner of the shed at any moment, but I don't look behind me.

I reach the top, the galvanized metal bites into my hands, and then I climb over.

I jump to the ground and run, dashing behind a monstrous hedge.

They will follow.

Already, I hear the clinking sounds as they climb the fence.

They won't find me though, if I can somehow reach Mary's house before the drug completely wipes me out. My left arm is now pretty much useless. I wonder how much time I have. Running probably makes it worse, but I can't let them get to me, not until I've figured out what is really going on.

CHAPTER 8

Mary lives on the second floor of an apartment building. It's a modest apartment, two bedrooms, a small kitchen, a small living and dining area. It suits her life, now.

The building itself is only four stories, just on the edge of downtown. Once, in the seventies, it was new, U-shaped, with a courtyard where the residents could have a barbeque or a party. Now, it's run-down, drab, and needs painting. Walkways line the inside of the U, and there are flights of stairs to each level.

I'm barely standing at the bottom of one of those flights of stairs, holding myself upright with my right hand. My left arm is numb, as is most of the left side of my body. It's been that way for a couple hours now. Either the drug they used in the darts wasn't dosed properly, or my body is doing a better job resisting it than Division Six had anticipated. It doesn't matter much.

At least I'm not about to become completely incapacitated any time soon.

The prospect of dragging myself up the stairs is daunting, but I have to do it. No one will do it for me, and the elevator, in the middle of the U, looks too far away.

I spent half the night getting here, avoiding Division Six. I don't want to spend another twenty minutes or more crossing the courtyard.

So up the stairs I go, one heave after another, using the flimsy rail to lean on as I drag my dead foot up behind me.

It takes me several minutes, but I eventually reach the top, elated that I have not toppled backwards or broken the railing.

Mary's door is two doors down.

I hobble my way down to it, then reach into my pocket for the key she insists I carry with me.

I enter the apartment, then shut the door behind me, locking it. I hope Joe has forgotten about Mary. I haven't talked about her in years, though I did mention her back when I was still mourning my old life. I can't remember if I ever mentioned her name, though.

It may not matter. Division Six probably knows about my past. I would be surprised if they didn't know that Mary was my girlfriend. I can only hope they think we lost contact.

And if they don't, I don't want to think about it.

I know I should leave, for her sake, but I don't have a choice thanks to that damned dart.

"Steve?"

Mary's voice. I woke her up.

"Yes, Mary," I say. "It's me."

"What are you doing here?" she asks. She hasn't emerged from the short hallway that leads to her bedroom, yet.

"I need a place to rest for a while," I say. I don't want to alarm her.

She shuffles out of the hallway, dressed in a violet colored night robe that has darker stitched flowers ringing the neck and running down the front. She wraps the belt around her waist and ties it off. Her eyes blink like she's still trying to clear the sleep from them, and her hair, normally a mass of dark curls atop her head, is crushed on one side from her pillow.

"Of course," she says. "It's been so long, I was beginning to wonder if you would come back."

It's been a year since the last time I saw her, maybe more. It's getting harder and harder for me to watch her age. If there was any way I could have given her some of my gifts, especially the one that was keeping me young, I would have done it long ago.

"It hasn't been that long," I say. "A year..."

"A year is a long time, Steve."

She crosses the room to where I am barely standing, then puts her arms around me. It feels good to be held by her, the heat of her just awake body warming my much colder one.

She steps back, a look of worry on her face. Her arms are still on me, though.

"What's wrong?" she asks. Her eyes are now open and clear, and she's fully awake.

"I've been drugged," I say. "I need a place to stay until it wears off."

"Drugged? I thought they didn't work on you."

"No, this is something else, not a normal drug."

My whole left side is now numb. I am not certain how long I can continue to stand.

"What then?"

I don't think it's a good idea to tell her, but I can tell already that she will badger it out of me. I've never been able to resist her.

I eye the couch.

"Would you mind if we sit, first?" I ask.

"Of course," she says.

She takes my hand, as if sensing I might have trouble walking the five feet to the couch, and leads me there. She tries to help me so that I don't fall into the couch, but I sit down hard, anyway. She's too slight to hold me up.

She keeps hold of my hand and sits down next to me.

"Now tell me," she says.

"Joe betrayed me," I say.

She draws in a deep breath, but says nothing. I have never really talked about Mary with Joe, but I've talked about Joe with Mary. She has always worried that Joe's experiments would turn for the worst.

"He's worked for the government for years, fed them information about me."

Now her expression changes, her mouth tightens up and her eyes narrow. Her hand squeezes mine tighter. Her anger is palpable.

"Why would he do that?" she asks.

"Money, unless he was working for them the whole time, but I don't think he was. I think they got to him some time after I met him."

"So he drugged you?"

"No. The government agents that tried to capture me did. Darts of some type, tranquilizers, I think. They put a dart in my shoulder."

"You didn't kill any of them, did you?" she asks. She knows I've killed people, before. I always claimed it was self defense. She doesn't know how I did it. I've never been able to tell her that.

I shake my head. Even that is getting difficult. I am going to be unable to stay awake much longer, I suspect. It seems I was wrong about its effects slowing down. The drug has started to work on my right side, too. It won't be long. I think it's speeding up.

"There were too many," I say. My tongue, of a sudden, feels thick. "All I could do was run."

Which is a shame. Absorbing one of them might have helped me clear the tranquilizers from my system.

"That's good," she says. "Maybe they won't chase you."

"No. They'll still chase me. This was their second attempt to capture me."

"Why?" she asks. There is alarm on her face, but she keeps it out of her voice.

"Joe said they were trying to protect me. He said someone was killing people like me."

Mary's face grows blurry. I blink, trying to clear my eyes, but all the blinking in the world is useless. It's the drug. If Division Six were to show up at Mary's door right now, I could do nothing to stop them from taking me.

"Mary," I say, "I think I'm staying the night."

Even to my ears, my words sound garbled.

Mary seems to understand.

"Of course, Dear. You can stay as long as you need."

Only until the drug clears, and then I'm going to see George.

But seeing George will have to wait.

CHAPTER 9

I wake up with my head in Mary's lap, her long, bony fingers stroking my hair. I wonder, momentarily, if she still sees me as a long lost lover, or if I am more like one of her children now, the wayward child who only comes home when he's in trouble.

I am not going to ask her, though. I don't really want to know the answer.

The room is lamp-lit. If the sun has come up, I cannot tell. She installed blackout curtains long ago for those times I might need a refuge. I'm not sure she's got her money's worth out of them. I've only stayed a few times.

"Mary," I say, my tongue still thick but intelligible, now, "how long?"

I hear a little intake of breath, but she doesn't stop stroking my hair. Maybe she still feels more lover than mother.

"A day and a half," she says. "I feared it would kill you."

"Joe was certain they wanted to capture me. I don't think it would have killed me."

"You didn't move for so long. Your breathing came to a near standstill."

Not surprising. Sleeping for me is akin to hibernation. I don't need as much air as before the change. I can hold my breath for twenty minutes or more without effort.

"It does that," I say.

"No, I've seen your sleeping before. You take a breath every three or four minutes. This was closer to ten minutes between breaths."

"The tranquilizer," I say.

"This was scary," she says. "I lost Bruce. I don't want to lose you, too."

I blink.

"It was so hard when Bruce died. I thought I would be all alone, but then you came back to me, and you hadn't changed. You were a gift from heaven to me. I thought, then, that I'd at least have you."

She continues to stroke my hair. I haven't had someone do that in so long, that I won't allow myself to move, even though I know it's probably time to leave.

"I loved you, you know," she says.

I turn my head to look up into her eyes. Blue flecked with gray, they looked down at me, wide and unflinching. I cannot remember her looking at me like that since we were young, nor any time since Bruce died, either. I hadn't let her get close enough, until now, for that.

"I loved you, too, but that was so..."

"Are you saying you don't love me anymore?" she says, interrupting me.

"No," I say. "Everything just changed. I changed."

"I never stopped, you know. You disappeared, everyone

thought you were dead, but I didn't believe it. I didn't want to believe it. I kept waiting for so long."

"You told me this before," I say.

A finger of hers rubs up against my ear. Once, it would have sent a shiver down my spine, but now, that sort of thing doesn't happen.

"I never ever stopped," she says.

And now, I get it.

I sit up, and her hand falls from my ear.

The content look she had on her face falters a little.

"It can't work," I say. "I'm not who I was."

"You don't know that. Just because you changed physically, it doesn't mean you've changed. You're still the Steve I loved. If you weren't, do you think I would let you keep coming around?"

"But you don't know..."

"What? I know you can't go out in the sunlight. I know you haven't changed in thirty years. And I know you don't suck blood, either."

While she's technically correct, she's wrong. Killing the way I do feeds me far better than any amount of food can. My kind would be a plague upon humans if we knew how to make more of us.

"I could help you," she says. "You wouldn't have to live out there on the streets. You could stay here."

"Not any more," I say. "Not while Division Six is after me."

I hear faint footsteps on the walkway outside.

"They won't find you here," she says. "I haven't told anyone about you."

I look into Mary's eyes, making it look like I'm thinking about how to respond, but I am actually listening to the footsteps as they approach her door, and then, without hesitation, continue past.

I almost sigh in relief, but manage to keep the sigh inside. Just because that person didn't stop at the door did not mean they weren't searching for me.

The footsteps are still audible to me in the distance. Mary can't hear them, but I whisper anyway. "That doesn't mean they don't know about you," I say. "They could have talked to people I knew in high school. They could come here looking to talk to you, wondering if you might know..."

By providence or luck, I pause there, long enough to hear the light tap-tick sound of someone trying to work the lock on Mary's front door.

"Steve," she says before I can clap my hand over her mouth.

The sounds in the lock stop for a moment, then resume.

I point at the door. I don't think she can hear the sounds, but she nods as if she understands.

I get to my feet as quietly as I can, thankful the couch is some synthetic fabric instead of leather, then tip-toe my way to the door.

The chain lock is slung to hold the door closed, which is a good thing, and the deadbolt is thrown, another good thing. I can keep the deadbolt from being opened, but if I do, whoever is trying to get in will just try to knock it down, or they'll give up and come through the window.

I put my foot against the base of the door to wedge it shut, then my ear up against the door to listen. I hear only the movement of the tools in the lock and the breathing of the man outside.

It *is* a man, or whoever it is breathes like one—too fast to be my kind. Besides, the stench is missing. I peek through the eye hole, but whoever is at the door is bent over, and I can't see them. I can't tell if it's Division Six, but I can't imagine they would work this way.

So if it's not Division Six, then...

Perhaps it's just a normal burglar that thinks everyone is asleep, but I don't believe that. The only other option that springs to mind is unpleasant—the man that's killing my kind, and somehow, he found me.

Mary gets off the couch and moves to the kitchen. She's pretty quiet for someone who doesn't spend her life hiding. She slings her purse over her shoulder.

The deadbolt unlocks. All that is left is the doorknob lock.

Mary reaches under the counter and pulls out a pistol. She steps out of the kitchen and approaches the door.

I shake my head and point to the back of the apartment. She has a window and a fire escape back there. If this is Division Six, they may take her, too, for what she knows about me. If this isn't...

She waves at me to come with her.

I nod and then wave her on. I want to turn out the lights, but she needs them to see where she's going.

I put my hand to the switch, and then she understands.

She turns and walks quickly to her room.

The doorknob lock springs open, and then the would-be intruder tries the knob.

The door pushes against my foot with a soft nudge. The would-be intruder is trying to be quiet. He must think we're asleep.

The intruder pushes harder, so that the door bows a bit at the top. He must know by now that it's the bottom that is stuck.

"Ste-eve, don't play with me," the intruder says in an eerie sing-song voice. A man—most definitely a man. And he knows my name.

He pushes harder, and it hurts my foot a little. The tennis shoe I am wearing is not good protection.

"Steve," says the intruder. "I know you're there. We have some things we need to talk about. I know what you are, and I know why Division Six wants you."

Could it be true? Or does he just want to get me to open the door and let him in?

"Who are you? Are you the killer?" I ask.

There is a slight pause before he answers. "Ah, so that's what they are saying about me?"

The pressure on the door eases.

"Are you?"

"I am no killer," he says. "I am a savior."

I hear the bedroom window open. The air starts to move around me.

"And if I don't want to let you in?"

"I'll have to force my way in," he says.

"Not much of a savior," I say.

"If I can't save you, I'll have to save everyone from you. I can't let Division Six take you."

A note in his voice advises caution. He's telling some of the truth, but not all of it.

"Your name, first," I say. Maybe I've heard of it.

"Max Hall," he says without hesitation.

I haven't heard the name before.

"Who do you work for, Max?"

"This isn't getting us anywhere, Steve. Let me in."

"You still haven't told me why I should let you in," I say.

I lean away from the door, but still hold my foot against it. By now, Mary should be off the fire escape.

"I can tell you things about yourself that you don't even know," he says. "I can tell you things that Joe and Division Six do not know."

My heart doesn't skip a beat, but panic flashes through my mind momentarily. He knows Joe, and he knows Joe works for Division Six.

"Tell me something I don't know, and I'll consider it."

"I know who made you," Max says.

"Bullshit," I say. No one knows how I became the way I did. It just happened.

I hear cars pull into the parking lot. A tire screeches.

"Ah, it looks like you've delayed too long. I'm coming in, now," Max says.

I pull away from the door just as a gun blast takes out the top hinge of the door. I don't know what kind of weapon Max is carrying that would take out the hinge on a steel door, but it's gone.

I run to the back room as another blast takes off the bottom hinge and the door falls open.

I look behind me and catch sight of Max as he enters the room. He's tall. Six foot five, at least. Short, dark hair tops a long face that's wearing reflective sunglasses. The gun he's carrying looks a lot like an oversized shotgun. A black sport coat tops a black shirt and black pants. A long knife hangs from his belt. I can imagine quite clearly what Max uses that knife for.

"Don't run, Steve. You'll only make things worse," he says.

"I'll take my chances," I say as I duck behind the wall.

The window stands open.

I jump through it just as a blast from that gun rips an enormous hole in the wall behind me.

I miss the fire escape, but the fall is only a story.

I land on my side, my left arm pinned awkwardly beneath me. It snaps, and an excruciating pain runs through my body.

Mary is right there to help me up, pulling at my other arm.

I cringe as I stand with her help. The arm hangs limply at my side, but I'm hardly worried about it. It will heal pretty quickly—a week at most.

"Run, Mary," I say.

No. I'm not worried about my arm.

Behind the apartment, there's a wall of trees, and on the other side, another apartment complex.

Mary doesn't run, though. She stands by my side.

I look up at the window I fell out of.

Max stands there.

"You're making a mistake," Max says.

He levels his gun at me.

"No," Mary says.

Her tiny gun is already aimed at Max.

She pulls the trigger and strikes Max in the shoulder just as his gun roars with a shot that misses to my left.

"Run!"

I take her arm with my right hand and pull her along behind me.

She hurt Max.

I don't think for a moment that will keep him from coming after me, and Division Six isn't about to stop, either.

CHAPTER 10

Mary and I cross a couple streets, then find a bus stop. We need to leave the area, and Mary's car is stuck in her apartment's parking lot with Division Six. There's no way we are going back there.

Fortunately, it's not so late that the buses have stopped running. One arrives after only three tense minutes of waiting for Max or Division Six to beat the bus.

My hope is that Division Six's appearance caused Max to put off hunting me for the moment, and that Max's presence will cause Division Six to forget about me for the same moment.

Still, I would have preferred the bus to have been waiting for us when we got to the bus stop.

Once we are on the bus, Mary pays the driver, and then follows me to the back seat. The bus is one of the articulated kind, and it's blissfully empty. The back seat is a long way from the driver, which should afford us a great deal of privacy.

My arm is killing me, and I take some time to poke around at it. After a few minutes of examination, I decide that it doesn't need to be set. Probably just cracks and not a break. They'll heal in a few days—less if I *take* someone.

I can't do that with Mary in tow.

Mary.

What am I going to do with her? She's a better shot than I would have given her credit for, but she doesn't deserve to be on the run with me. I can already feel the guilt for ruining her life a second time, the first being when I disappeared on her thirty years ago.

I look up at her, and she's visibly shaking. Now that we have a moment to rest, her body is reacting to the stress.

"I'm sorry, Mary," I say. "I shouldn't have come to your home."

Her body stops shaking for a moment as she looks at me.

"You're sorry?" she asks. "Where else would you have gone? Don't blame yourself for this, Steve. Blame the assholes that are following you. Blame the guys who are shooting at you."

"But you don't deserve..."

She cuts me off.

"Don't you tell me what I deserve." Her voice rings with a strange mix of anger and hysteria. "I'll make that decision myself. You hardly even know me. You show up once a year or so, and won't let me get close to you. You don't know what I deserve."

We sit in silence for a moment. I look up, can see the driver of the bus glancing in his mirror. Mary's voice must have carried all the way to him.

"You're right," I say.

"Glad you understand that. Now, where are we going?"

"Wherever this bus is going," I say. "Past a few more stops, and then we'll get off and find our way to George's house."

"Your ex-cop friend?"

"Yes."

"You sure he hasn't been betraying you like Joe?" she asks.

"No," I say, "but I have to find out."

Mary frowns, then says, "I suppose you do."

CHAPTER 11

The bus trip takes us most of the rest of the night, three different transfers, and a long layover at one stop after the last bus of the night. As a result, we don't get to George's place until about a half hour before dawn.

Mary looks exhausted, and I'm feeling worn out, too, with the healing of my arm taking much of my energy. I need food, Mary needs sleep.

"Steve," George says as he opens the door.

He's a large man, a half-foot taller than me, and spreading ever since he retired from police work. His hair mostly disappeared long ago, and the first few liver spots are starting to show on his scalp. But a genuine smile spreads across his face, one that I often see when I appear at his door, and surprising to see on a man who has spent so much time dealing with the darker half of society.

"Who's this you've got with you?" George asks.

"This is Mary," I say.

George extends his hand in greetings and says, "Mary, it's nice to meet you."

Mary takes George's hand, but then drops it almost immediately. She's too tired to do much more.

"We need a place to stay for the day," I say.

"You know you're always welcome, Steve," he says, and steps back out of the doorway.

I give Mary a little push to get her going, and then follow her through the door.

"A rough night?" George asks as the door shuts behind me.

"A rough couple days," I say.

"Days? What could give you rough days?"

"Someone betrayed me," I say. I am suddenly unsure of whether or not I can trust George. As an ex-cop, he might feel differently than I expect about Division Six.

"Do I know them?" George asks.

He puffs up a little, thinking, I'm sure, about protecting me. He's always had a thing for protecting me, even when he was a cop.

"I don't think so," I say. I don't remember ever telling him about Joe

"How did they betray you?"

Mary chose that moment to stumble, and I went to her to help her up. I used my right arm, trying to hide my injury from George. I don't know if he's noticed yet.

"How about we discuss this after we find her a bed," I say. I do want to get her to bed, but I'm also hoping to buy myself time to figure out what side of the fence George might fall on. I know he won't want me dead, but if he gets the idea that the government is trying to protect me, he might help them. Unless he knows already, and has betrayed me to them like Joe. In that case, coming here was a big mistake and I was done for when I knocked on the door.

"The spare bedroom," George says. "You'll have to sleep on the couch, or something."

"I'll take the floor in Mary's room," I say.

"Just point me to the room," Mary says. "I can get there."

"Up the stairs, on the right at the end of the hall," George says. "I keep it for Steve, so it'll stay dark all day. You won't wake until you want to."

"Thanks," she says, and turns the corner to head up the stairs.

George's house is a typical split level home. The bedrooms are up the stairs to my right. To my left, on the same floor as the entryway, are the kitchen and living room. George has the floor below set up as an entertainment room. The life of a bachelor with money.

I followed Mary up the stairs with my eyes, and waited until she turned into the room before I turned back to George.

"She's nice," George says, "though a little older than I thought you'd go for."

"She was my girlfriend before all this happened to me," I say. "We're the same age."

George laughs. "I should have known. Is she single?"

I nod.

"You mind if I ask her out for coffee?"

I'm struck by my inability to answer his question. I don't have any right to her, and I know she would be better off with George, or any other normal person, but I just can't say yes. I don't want to.

"Maybe after this is all over," I say.

"Hey thanks!" he says, then slaps my broken arm.

I grunt in pain and pull away from him.

"Hey," George says. "What's up with the arm?"

"Broke it jumping out a window."

"It'll heal?" he asks. He knows I can't go to a doctor.

"Yeah. Just cracks, I think."

"Then let's go have a drink while you tell me how your last couple nights got so rough that you're jumping out of windows."

He leads me down the stairs into his entertainment room. A large black-leather sectional sofa hugs one wall, and a pool table dominates the center of the room. There's a pinball machine, a couple of old arcade games, and, most importantly, his wet bar.

George steps behind the bar while I head to the sofa.

"You want one?" George asks. He always asks.

"A drink? No thanks," I say. It would be a waste. Alcohol hasn't affected me since the change, and mostly, it doesn't taste good anymore, either.

I sit down in the couch and sink into it. It molds itself around me like a fine leather coat.

George finishes mixing his drink, more than likely a Jack and Coke, then walks over to sit on the other leg of the couch. He leans forward and puts his shoulders on his knees, holding his drink between them.

"Now," he says, "spill."

I stare at his drink for a moment, pondering whether I can trust him. I had trusted Joe and had been wrong. George, as a police officer, had been a government employee at one time. Was he still? Had he *retired* so he could keep an eye on me?

I don't think I have much of a choice, though.

"First, I need to ask you something, and I'd like you to try to not be offended."

"You know I'm not offended easily," he says.

"I know, but this..."

"Just ask me, already," George says.

I take a breath.

"You aren't still working for the government, are you? You're really retired."

He sits up.

"I'm really retired," he says, as earnest a look on his face as I had seen. "I get my pension check, and that's it."

"You aren't reporting about me to anyone?"

"No."

He doesn't seem to be lying.

"Have you ever?"

"No."

He sets the drink aside, planting it on a gold plated coaster. He seems to be understanding how serious this is.

"If I find out you are betraying me like Joe did..."

I let the implication hang in the air between us.

He didn't rise to the bait, though. Instead, he seized on the one piece of information I let slip.

"Joe? You mean that scientist guy who's been trying to help you for twenty years? He was working for the government?"

I guess I had told him about Joe.

I nod. I should have realized he would put my questions together and figure out what was going on. He spent forty-some years as a cop.

He looks me straight in the eye.

"I swear, Steve, that I haven't told a soul about you. Not even when you took that bullet for me so long ago. You asked me not to, and I didn't. You are the one constant in this ex-cop's life, and I wouldn't destroy that for anything. I would die before I snitched on you."

Good enough for me.

I tell him about Joe. Everything. I tell him about my encounter with Division Six in the tunnel, my escape from Division Six at Joe's house, and then the odd encounter at the apartment with Max Hall.

"You think this Max Hall guy is the one that Joe was talking about?"

"I think it's possible, though with some of the things he said, I have to wonder whether he was just trying to get me to open the door so he could kill me, or if he really did want to help me escape Division Six."

"I think you made the right choice," George says. "They're both telling you the other isn't to be trusted."

"And there was Taggart," I say.

"Taggart?"

"The one like me that warned me to run in the tunnel," I say.

"Yes." His lips tighten up. "That is curious."

"What do you think I should do?" I ask.

Now, George sits back in his couch, rubs his balding pate, then reaches for his neglected drink. He takes a few sips while he thinks.

I close my eyes while I wait for him to cogitate. Behind my eyelids, the scene in Joe's garage plays back, repeatedly showing me the expression he wore just before I knocked him out. I can't tell if the sorrow I saw there was because he truly felt bad that he had betrayed me, or if he felt it because he got caught. I wonder if he has any sense of what he has done to me. I begin to think that maybe, after this is all over, I will go back to him and have a more in depth conversation. I still feel a rent in my heart that I hadn't thought possible. Not knowing why is its own torture, and I won't be able to rest until I understand.

"I think," George says, interrupting my thoughts, "that you need a place to lay low for a few days so that arm can heal, and then you have to find a place for Mary. They'll be looking for her, hoping she will lead you to them. After that, maybe you need to disappear, move to another city."

"Move?" I ask. "But you? Mary?"

"You'll have to part with us eventually," George says. "You'll outlive us both. What's it matter if it's now or later?"

"I don't know other cities," I protest. "What would I do there?"

"What do you do here?"

He has a point. I don't do much of anything here, not since the *change*. I still don't want to go. Just the idea is terrifying.

"They'll follow me," I say.

George sits forward again.

"Promise me that you won't get offended by what I'm going to say."

"How can I promise that?"

"Promise me then that you'll at least keep an open mind."

"I'll try," I say.

"Good enough."

He inhales, then says, "You haven't been living since I've known you, not on your own, at least. You sleep wherever you sleep, you get handouts from your Mary, me, and Joe. You haven't moved on. You need to start your life again, Steve."

I tell myself I'm not offended. I'm not at all sure my attempt is working.

"You don't want me here anymore?" I ask. "You want me to go?"

"No, I don't want you to go. I want you safe. I want you living your life, not sleeping in sewers or under bridges. You're better than that."

"I was." Long ago, before the change. "Now, I'm just a freak, a monster, even. I've killed people, and you know it. I've taken their energy, used it to heal myself."

"You haven't done that in years," he says.

"No." Not that I will admit to him. Sometimes, things happen on the streets. It's always self defense, at least since I met George.

"You could move to another city, get a job..."

"I can't get a job," I say. "They always interview during the day, even for night jobs. I can't go to those interviews."

"You're just wallowing in self-pity," he says. "This trouble you're in is a wake-up call. How long has Joe worked to find a way to change you back?"

"Twenty-two years," I say. But after learning of his association with the government, I wonder if that was really his goal.

"And he hasn't succeeded in all that time. You're going to have to face the fact that you're not going to ever go back to your old life. Your parents are dead, your friends are all thirty years older than you appear to be. You need a purpose, Steve."

It's hard to listen to him. I want to shut him up, tune him out, but his words are making it through. He's right. I know it. But I don't like it, and I'm comfortable with the life I had worked out for myself. It was working, until Joe betrayed me.

"Did you hear me, Steve?"

I don't think he trusts that I haven't tuned him out.

"I heard you," I say, "but I need time to think."

CHAPTER 12

I spent the night sleeping in the room with Mary, though I didn't climb into the bed with her. I slept on the floor. I'm used to sleeping on hard surfaces—you haven't experienced it until you've slept on the brick walkway in an old sewer—the carpet of the room is a down-filled mattress in comparison to most of the places I sleep.

Now I'm awake, and Mary still sleeps. My broken arm aches, but I can already tell that it's healing. Three days, maybe four, and it will be back to normal. It's not quite the regeneration you see in movies, but it serves me a lot better than not having the ability at all.

I sit up.

Mary's head faces me, her eyes twitch beneath her eyelids in the clutches of a dream. I hope it's not about last night. I don't want her dreaming about that.

Maybe George is right. If I stay here, I put her in danger—I put George in danger. I could go to another city, find something I could do for money and rent an apartment, some little dive of a place, and start making something of myself.

But the thought of it terrifies me.

Mary's lips twitch, then pull down in a frown.

Now I'm certain her dream is about last night.

I can't beat the government.

And I can't let her get hurt because of me.

I'm just not sure about where to go.

It needs to be a big city, a place where I can hide, where it won't seem strange that I never come out during the day. Ideally, it will be far enough away that Division Six will not even think of looking for me there.

Shit. If I'm really going to go somewhere else, I should get out of the country. Canada would be easiest, but it's likely the easiest place for Division Six to reach. Maybe Europe would be better. A place like London, or maybe Paris. But I don't have the money to get there.

And the passport problem. How do I get one? I don't have a driver's license, let alone access to my birth certificate, or any other form of ID. Hell, no one will believe my birth certificate, anyway, even if I could show up at a licensing station.

In order to leave the country, I'll need to get fake documents. Hell, even to get a job, I'll need fake documents.

"Dammit," I say.

"What?" Mary asks.

She's looking at me. I don't know how long she's been looking, or if I woke her by speaking. It's dark enough in here that I'm not at all sure she can see me. There is enough light seeping past the curtains that she might be able to.

She takes away any chance that she can't see me by

reaching over and turning on the silver desk lamp that's George's idea of a bedside lamp.

"I'm thinking it's time for me to leave Seattle, Mary, and go somewhere they won't find me."

"That's probably a good idea," she says.

I expected her to say anything but that.

"So why are you swearing?" she asks.

"I don't have any documents. I can't get a passport or a driver's license. No one will believe I'm the person that belongs to my birth certificate. I can't pay for fake documents, and wouldn't know where to get them if I could."

"I would give you the money," she says.

"I know. You're too good to me. I still wouldn't know where to get them. But that's not the only problem."

She sits up in bed and pulls the covers up around her, hiding her body from me. Her hair is a mess, but it's a beautiful mess. It reminds me of the times before my change when we would wake up next to each other and talk until we were late for our morning classes.

"What other problems are there?" she asks.

"I won't know anyone," I say. "I won't know where the safe places to sleep are, I won't know where I can get food, and getting wherever I go will pose a problem, too."

"The daylight," she says.

I nod.

She looks toward the window, covered with blackout curtains (care of George). She probably wishes she could see out.

A couple minutes pass that way, me watching her watch the window. There are lines on her face, lines that weren't there when we were dating so long ago. In a way, her face is more attractive to me with them than the memory of her without them is. I want to go over to her, climb in bed next to her like I used to, and caress her face with my fingertips.

But I can't let that happen. I can't allow myself to take anything more from her than I already have.

She turns away from the window and looks at me with fierce brown eyes.

"I'll go with you," she says.

"No," I say. I can't spit the word out of my mouth fast enough. "I can't put you in any more danger than you are already in."

"I can't go back to my apartment," she says. "I can't go back to that life. Your government friends will be waiting there for me, and they'll make me tell them about you, and I won't do that."

"But, you can just hide for a few days, or a couple weeks," I say.

"You think they won't wait for me? There will be someone watching my apartment until I return. And you need my help," she says.

I don't like sitting on the floor and talking to her about this, so I get to my feet. Now that I'm looking down on her, I don't feel any more comfortable than I did sitting on the floor looking up.

I cross to the bed and sit on the end of it.

"I've already made a mess of your life," I say. "Isn't that enough? I owe you, not the other way around."

She smiles at me, leans forward, and reaches out to touch me lightly on the cheek with her fingertips. The covers slip a little, exposing a nipple. I don't think she notices. I haven't seen them in so long, it's hard not to look.

"You're right," she says. Her breast slopes down, just a little, the result of nursing her children. "You do owe me, and you're going to repay that debt by taking me with you and letting me help, wherever it is that you go."

"But…"

She puts a fingertip to my lips.

"No, listen. I loved you, and you left, and I was hurt for a long time. I had dreams with you, and I never got to fulfill any of them. When you came to me after Bruce died, I thought that God had given me another chance with you. You hadn't changed, and it was like I would get to start over.

"But then you never let yourself get close like we were before, and you would disappear again for months at a time. I've lived with that these last years because it's what I had, and I told myself I was content with it."

She places her other hand on my other cheek, dropping the sheet entirely. Her fingers are warm, the heat from her body is just palpable on my skin.

"I'm not content with it," Mary says. "I'm not content with it at all. I want to be with you, whatever happens. I want you back."

The conflict within me threatens to split me apart. It has been so long since I was with a woman, so long since I was with Mary. It will be so easy to give in to her, to let her help me, but if she stays with me, her life is in danger, far more than mine. She can't regenerate anything.

"I just don't want to see you hurt," I say.

"Where would you be if you hadn't come to me?" she asks.

She has a point. I would probably be dead by now, Max's giant knife having severed my head from my body as I slept off the effects of the Division Six tranquilizer. Or, Division

Six would have found me and I'd be a rat in a laboratory experiment.

Which is what I was for the last thirty years with Joe. A rat in his experiments.

"Nowhere good," I say. "But that doesn't matter. I still don't want you to come with me. I don't want you hurt."

"And you think that your leaving me again won't hurt?"

It will. I know it, now, if I did not know it before. And it will hurt me, too. I don't want to leave the only friends I have, but I'm the one putting them in danger just by being me.

"What about your kids, Mary? If you leave with me, it could put them in danger. Division Six could look to them to try to find you, or Max could."

Her hands fall away from my face to land in her lap.

"They wouldn't..."

"Do you want to take the risk? We have no idea who Max or Division Six really work for, or what they might do. If I leave, and they want to find me bad enough, they will follow every lead, and that will lead them to your children."

She sits on the bed, quietly wringing her hands.

I watch her eyes, looking for any hint as to what she's thinking. They seem to be pleading with me to make what I said not true, but it is true. The people hunting me may not go that far, but if I were them, I would.

Eventually, she looks down, then pulls the blanket up around her again.

"All right," she says. "You win, but when it's all over, you know where I live. Send me a message or a letter, and I'll come to you."

"I will," I say, knowing my promise is empty. How will I

know when they've given up? Any attempt to contact her after I've left might lead them back to me.

And then we stare at each other, me wishing she hadn't covered up, wishing that we could lie together one more time before I leave her forever.

Neither of us say another word until George knocks at the door.

"Rise and shine, you two," he says. "The sun's going down, and I've got breakfast cooking."

CHAPTER 13

"I'm going," I say just after we all sit down at George's table to plates of eggs and bacon, "but I'll need some help, George."

"Of course. What do you need?" George asks after swallowing a bite of his eggs.

"ID. Money. A car."

"You're not asking for much," he says as he plops another bite into his mouth.

My own eggs are sitting in front of me, untouched, so far. Mary is testing a piece of bacon with her tongue—it's more than just a bit crispy. George seems to like his bacon burnt.

"I know it's a lot to ask..."

"I didn't say I wouldn't do it," he says around his eggs. He swallows. "The ID will be the tricky part. I worked the other side of the law from the people that could get you those things. I know who many of the best are, but they'll clam up if they see me coming, if they are still in business. It's been a few years. The money and the car aren't big problems, once we have the ID. You'll want the car registered to the name on the ID, of course. You'll probably need a few thousand bucks, too, to pay first and last wherever you set up."

"You don't have to give me that much," I say, aghast at the amount of money he's talking about. I had been thinking a few hundred for gas and food.

"You'll need it," he says, "and I owe it to you."

"You don't owe me anything."

"Don't be an idiot," he says, shaking his head. "You took that bullet for me all those years ago, and if you hadn't, I'd be dead now. Everything I have today is something I wouldn't have if it weren't for you, and over the years, you haven't asked for much except for a meal and the occasional overnight in my bedroom. I'll give you whatever I damn well please, and you'll take it without complaining."

I wait a few moments to see if he will say more, and once I decide he will say nothing else, I say, "Thank you."

There's little else I can say.

I dip my fork into my eggs for the first time and scoop a large clump into my mouth. They're good, if a little flat, but food has tasted flat to me since the change, so it's nothing unexpected. They don't taste bad, just not satisfying.

"I can help with money," Mary says.

"No," I say simultaneously with George.

"Why not?"

"If Division Six is watching your house, they'll be watching your bank accounts and your credit cards. They'll be looking for you to surface somewhere, and a big money draw will certainly lead them to think you are helping me."

"Steve is right," George says. "They'll be looking at all of those things in their effort to find him."

Mary frowns, disappointed she can't help. She must feel trapped here because of me. The only recourse is to get out as fast as I can.

I decide to return to the ID problem. "So, if the ID will be tricky, what's our first step?"

"The first step is to make some calls, and then visit a couple of people if I have any luck. You get to stay here until I come back. Don't leave the house, don't make phone calls. I'd suggest you do some research on your destination, but I don't want to see traces of it in my computer. I don't want to have any idea where you're going, just in case they trace you here."

Great. I'm going to have to go to my destination blind, wherever that destination ends up being.

CHAPTER 14

It takes two days for George to find an ID man. I spend those two days talking with Mary and healing. There are times during our discussions where I find myself starting to waver on my conviction that I should leave her behind, but I lock down those thoughts as soon as I recognize they are happening. I don't want her to notice.

Once he's found his man, George takes a picture of me, brings it to the guy, and a day later, I have a passport, a driver's license, and a social security card. They all share the same name, and it's not my own. The passport and the driver's license have my picture on them, but the name says Aaron Andrews.

"I thought they would have my name on them," I say when George brings them to me.

"That's not a good idea," he says. "They'll be searching for your name to pop up, and when it does, they'll investigate. Better to change it."

"I guess I can live with it. I wish you would have given me a choice on the name," I say.

"No such luck. Had to match the name on the social security card."

"How does that work?" I ask.

"I don't know. I was told that it's valid and you won't run into any issues with using it."

"That doesn't sound promising," I say.

Mary reaches over and takes the driver's license from me.

"Aaron," she says, looking up at me. "I could get used to that."

I turn to George.

"So, the car?"

"I've got a line on one. An SUV with blacked out windows. You can hang a curtain or something to keep the light out in case you have to sleep in it."

"When?"

"I'll pick it up tomorrow," he says.

"And then I can go."

"Yes. Then you can go. You *are* still going, aren't you?"

I nod.

"You've decided where to go?"

I nod again, even though I haven't. I'm torn between heading north to Canada, and heading across the country to someplace like New York or Boston. Either way, I'm starting to look forward to the trip, to something new. Leaving Mary and George will be hard, but with time to think about it, the idea of making these changes, forced as they are, seems to have brought me a little energy.

A forceful knocking at the front door makes us all look at each other. It's after ten at night. No one should be knocking at the door.

"They've found me," I say.

"You don't know that," he says, but there is a nervous tremor in his voice.

"Hide, Mary," I say.

"You, too," George says.

"No. I need to see who it is."

Mary is still standing there when the person at the door knocks again.

"Mary, go!" I say, pushing her.

She turns and leaves to head down the stairs to the lower level and the possible escape route of the rear door, but she's looking back toward me as she takes her first steps.

George also turns away from me, but he heads to the front door. Before he opens it, he reaches into the drawer of a side table and takes out a pistol. He's not taking any chances.

I stay in the kitchen, but hide my body behind a corner. I can peek around the corner to see who is at the door.

George opens the door, but doesn't open it wide enough for me to see who is there.

"Hello?" he says.

"Hi," says a voice I recognize from that first night. Taggart. "I was hoping you could help me."

"Help you?" George asks. He has his gun hidden behind his back.

"I'm looking for someone. Not quite as tall as you, dark hair, and about twenty-five years old. Goes by the name of Steve."

"Don't know anyone like that," George says.

"You sure you haven't seen him? A neighbor of yours says he saw someone like that come to your door a few nights ago."

I don't remember seeing any of his neighbors outside as we walked the half-mile from the bus stop, but I suppose they might have seen us. He didn't mention Mary, though, so maybe he is just probing for a reaction.

And then I realize that the stench of my kind is not with him this time, either. It doesn't make sense, and I want to ask him about it. I know he's like me, but the stench should be there.

"No. No one came to my door," George says.

"Well, if you see him, could you tell him that Taggart from Division Six is looking for him? Tell him that it's not official business, and that I'd really like to see him. I've got some information for him."

"If I see someone named Steve," George says, "I'll be sure to tell him that, but I hardly leave my house these days. Sorry I couldn't be of more help."

"Yeah, so am I," Taggart says. Then he starts yelling through the door. "Steve, they're searching for you. I won't tell them you're here, but they'll find you soon enough, anyway."

I step out from behind the wall.

"Wait! Let him in, George."

"What are you doing?" George asks.

"I need some questions answered," I say.

George scowls at me, thinking, I'm sure, that I am making a huge mistake, but Taggart is the only one of these people I trust—he protected me that first night, at risk to himself. George pulls open the door, despite his concern, and Taggart strides into the room, his huge frame taking up most of the doorway, just like he had in the tunnel.

His hair is longer than shoulder-length, but I cannot

tell how long. His eyebrows are bushy, his face weathered and pockmarked like I remember, but it would have been that way before the change—it didn't get that way, after. He's wearing a long, dark, leather coat and has a dark red, button-down shirt on beneath it. Black jeans only add to the intimidation factor that the rest of his outfit and his size portray.

George shuts the door behind him.

"You said you have some information for me," I say.

"I do," he says. "They've mobilized everyone to look for you. This was a good place to hide, but there are still tracks for them to find. I covered up what I could, but I couldn't erase it all. They would find the holes in the data if I did that, and it would lead them here just as easily. You have to leave."

"I am leaving. How did you find me here?"

"I found mention of you in several police reports. Nothing that tied you and your friend here directly, but he was the only cop that left thumbprints, both digital and otherwise, on all of those reports. It seemed like he might have been looking out for you."

Of course he was. I glance over at George, and he's got a look of dismay on his face.

"How did you get into those files?" George asks.

"Division Six has access, and it's my job to get into those things, but that's enough of that. You said you have questions, Steve. Ask. We don't have much time before they begin to wonder where I am."

"Why can't I smell the scent," I ask.

"They *fixed* me," he says.

I think he sees my hopes go up on my face.

"No, no," he says. "I'm not fixed permanently. It's some sort of gene therapy that they're using. It has the side effect of limiting the stench. It makes it so that I can stand the light just a little better, limits the pain, but the therapy has a limited duration. A week or so, at best, before it wears off and I have to spend another three hours in a chair getting fed drugs through an IV, and those drugs cause excruciating pain while they're entering my body."

He pulls up his sleeve and shows me his wrist. He has an IV shunt permanently embedded, but the skin around it is a pale yellow-green color.

"Your body is trying to reject the shunt," I say.

"Yes," he says. "The drugs help with that, too."

"Still, it must be worth it," I say, "otherwise, you wouldn't do it."

"It might be worth it if I had a choice."

"You have a choice, don't you?"

He shakes his head once, more like a twitch.

"Not any more. Do you have other questions? I need to get a move on before they figure out where I am."

He obviously does not want to answer more questions about the drugs—my only guess is that something terrible took place when they brought him in. I suspect they didn't give him a choice.

"Why did you warn me, there, in the tunnel?" I asked.

"They were going to take you, make you like me. The thing is, once you work for them, you don't control your own life any longer. They watch everything you do."

I think it's a little too late for that warning. They've been watching me for years.

"Why do they want me? Joe told me someone is killing

everyone like us, and that Division Six is only trying to protect me."

"He lies," Taggart says. "Division Six is the danger to you."

"Then what about Max Hall?"

Taggart's eyes sharpen on the mention of Max's name. He knows who Max is.

"How do you know that name?" Taggart asks.

"He came to the door of a place I was staying," I say. I leave out mention of Mary because I do not know if Taggart knows she is involved, yet.

"You talked to him," Taggart says.

"Yes. He said he knows who made me. He tried to talk me into letting him in, and when I refused, he broke down the door and tried to kill me."

"I have to go," he says, and turns to leave.

"Wait. You know him. Who is he? What does he want with me?"

Taggart turns back to me, indecision on his face. And then his eyes stop shifting, indicating he has come to a decision.

"Don't trust everything Max says, but trust this. If he's trying to kill you, he will keep at it until he succeeds."

Taggart turns, squeezes past George, puts his hand to the doorknob, and turns it.

"How do you know him?" I ask before the door cracks open.

Taggart looks back at me.

"Max used to work for Division Six," Taggart says, then slips out the door into the night before I can wrap my mind around his statement.

CHAPTER 15

Drugs, salvation, damnation. All these things run through my mind as I stare at the door through which Taggart had left.

And Max Hall had been a Division Six operative.

But now, he's either a rogue killer, or he's my savior, like he had claimed at one point. In either case, it seems he's a very big thorn in Division Six's side.

And the more I think about the reaction on Taggart's face after the mention of Max's name, the more I think there is a personal connection between them. Max had been important in Taggart's life.

"I'll get the car in the morning," George says. "I don't think you can wait any longer."

"Right."

But my thoughts aren't on the car, or on escaping. Instead, I'm bent on figuring out the entanglements between Max Hall and Division Six, and I haven't any idea where to start. I don't have enough evidence to come to any conclusions, but I can't leave it alone.

I'm tempted to search him out before I leave.

But that's a ridiculous idea. He may think he needs to kill me, and I'm not that interested in dying. At the same time, I can't help but be curious as to *why* Division Six is working on drugs to *fix* us, and Max might know.

And there's that other thing he said back at Mary's apartment. "I know who made you," he said. Could it be true? Did someone make me? Had someone done this to me, like some secret government experiment?

Was it Division Six?

"Are you all right?" George asks. He's looking at me as if I'm doing something strange.

"What? Yes, I'm fine. I was just thinking," I say.

"About?"

"About what Taggart said. I wish he had given me more time. The more I think about what he said, the more questions I have." I'm not sure I want to mention my thoughts about Max. If I decide to search him out, I don't want George trying to talk me out of it.

"Okay. I'm off to bed. I need some sleep if I'm going to get that car in the morning."

"Good night," I say, and then George heads up the stairs to his bedroom.

I head downstairs, to where Mary had hidden herself.

I find her sitting on one of George's bar stools. She's been waiting for me, it seems.

"So that guy that tried to barge his way into my apartment worked for Division Six?" she asks.

I nod. "Seems that way."

I pull out the stool next to her and sit on it, leaning against the bar counter.

"And this Taggart guy? He's like you?"

"Did you hear it all?" I ask.

"Most of it," she says.

"Then you know about the drugs."

"It sounds like they could make you almost normal."

"It does. It doesn't sound pleasant, though."

She reaches her hand out so that her fingertips brush my arm where it rests on the bar top.

"What will you do?" she asks.

"I'm still leaving," I say.

"Without me?"

I'm surprised she brought that up again.

"I thought that was already decided."

"It is," she says. "That doesn't mean I want you to leave without me."

"Mary, we talked about this. Your family..."

"Shhh. I know. But Taggart's visit got me thinking. If he can find you here, Division Six will find you here. This Max Hall guy will find you. They'll know I was here. And George..." She trails off, leaving the air full of implications.

I'm getting an inkling of what she is thinking. I don't like it.

If I leave, and George and Mary don't disappear with me, who knows what Division Six will do to them?

"Division Six might not do anything to the two of you," I say.

"You can't be certain," she says. "What about Max? He's ready to kill you. If he finds us, would he hesitate to use us against you?"

I don't know the answers, but I know the questions will haunt me, even after I leave, unless I do something first to allay them.

"Mary," I say, "you should get some rest."

I can see her eyes narrow in the dim glow of the replica bar lights that hang over the pool table.

"Why? I'm not tired, yet."

"Please," I say, "I need to think, and you need rest if you are going to drive us out of here tomorrow."

I hate myself for planting the thought in her head that I've given in to her, but she just might have to do that. Division Six, if they find out I'm here, might try to take me down in the middle of the day.

"You mean I'm going with you?"

I nod. "At least as far as the next state," I say. And I'm somewhat surprised to find that I mean it. "We'll leave as soon as George is back with the van."

She looks a little disappointed, but I can see hope there, a hope that didn't exist moments before. It lifts my heart, just a little, to see the hope on her face. I wonder, when the time comes, if I will be able to leave her.

She leans in to me and plants a kiss on my cheek. Her lips are warm. I feel like she thought about a more intimate kiss, but decided to play it safe. I'm disappointed.

"Thank you," she says.

Then she climbs off her stool, her fingers trail down my arm until they are no longer touching me, and then she climbs the stairs, leaving me alone in George's parlor.

CHAPTER 16

I wait until I hear the door shut upstairs, until I know that Mary's going to bed, before I cross the room to the gun safe that George keeps next to the dartboard. I know that most of the time, he doesn't keep it locked—a serious failing for an ex-cop—living alone as he does. And when I pull at the handle, the door swings open.

There are a pair of rifles and a shotgun hanging inside, and at the bottom, a rather large, mean-looking handgun. Says Desert Eagle on the side. That should do the trick. There's a magazine next to it.

I pick up the gun, check that the safety is on, then pick up the magazine and examine it. It's full.

I take the gun and the magazine upstairs, rummage through the closet until I find one of George's coats that I can wear. It's a bit oversized, but it has large pockets—large enough that the gun will fit in one of them. I slip the gun into one pocket, the magazine into the opposite pocket, and then I put the coat on. It's a bit large for me, but it'll do. I slip my new identity into one of its pockets, just in case.

I put my hand to the doorknob, and then pause for a moment, suspended.

It strikes me that I might be making a mistake. Leaving the house puts me at the mercy of whatever is out there. Division Six might find me. Max might find me.

But if Taggart reports where I am, Division Six will find me here.

And Max. If Max finds me, he's the one I want to talk to. I need to find out if he's just blowing smoke up my ass about knowing who made me.

Who made me?

I've grown so used to thinking that the change was something natural that happened to me, crazy as it is, that even the idea that someone *made* me seems strange. I have to know, which means I have to find Max.

But finding Max within the city at night? Max could be anywhere. He could be in his bedroom at his motel, though I don't think he will be. He'll be out there looking for me, just like Division Six is.

But I'm not going to sit here all night waiting for them to come to me.

I open the door and slip out into the night.

They sky is dark with clouds. No moon to illuminate me, no stars, either. Just streetlamps. It feels a bit like it might rain, but that doesn't bother me.

At the end of George's driveway, I pause for a moment and look around. I stand just outside the pool of light that the closest streetlamp splays on the ground. The houses across the street are all dark, except for the one two doors down. The owner of that house likes to keep his yard lights on all the time. I've never seen them off.

What I don't see is any indication that Max or Division Six are here. No black vehicles, no people walking about in the shadows.

So far, Taggart hasn't told anyone he found me.

The place to start looking, I guess, is Mary's apartment. Division Six will be there, waiting. Maybe Max will be there, too.

I step out into the dark, skirting the pools of light, and make my way to the bus stop. It's still early enough, I'll be able to catch a bus to Mary's. I'll have a wait once I get there—the first bus back won't arrive until something like four in the morning, but it will give me time.

At the bus stop, the lights that illuminate the covered waiting area flicker as if they don't really want to be on. I hang back in the darkness, leaning against a tree. I don't want to expose myself to whoever might be watching, not until the bus is just about to arrive.

The flickering light plays games with my vision and I know it will start to give me a headache if I have to stand here too long, but I don't have a choice. I need to watch for the bus. I don't want it to pass me by because I'm hiding back here by the tree.

Minutes pass. A few cars drive by, but not the bus. I slip my hands into my pockets. The gun is there, a cold piece of metal with death as its only purpose. I haven't held a gun in years, haven't fired one in longer. I brought it for protection, but now, it's starting to feel just like a weight.

The weight of it sparks questions. Should I really be doing this? Is it realistic that Max will be at Mary's? Division

Six will be there, I'm sure, but Max? Max won't be there. He'll be out looking for me, searching my haunts. He won't be waiting for me to show up at a place that's under the watch of Division Six.

I see lights in the distance, widely spaced. The big windows. The bus.

It's time to go, but something holds me up.

I want to know these things. I want to know who did this to me, if, indeed, someone did this to me. But knowing won't change me back, and tomorrow, I start a new life somewhere else, a better life.

The interior of the bus is lit. I can see it's mostly empty. I take a step toward it.

But no, this whole idea is ridiculous.

The bus passes by the bus stop, taking with it any chance of going to Mary's tonight.

And as I watch it disappear into the night, I realize I've made the right decision. *Why* doesn't matter so much as protecting my friends and protecting myself. Escaping.

It's time to go back to George's, and in the morning, we leave.

I turn away from the bus stop and take two steps before I collide with the barrel of a gun.

CHAPTER 17

The barrel of the gun is in my chest, pressed against the coat. The man holding it is taller than me, taller than George, has a clean shaven face and a crooked hook of a nose, obviously broken somewhere in his past. His hair is cut short, but not buzzed. It sticks up at odd angles like the man rolled out of bed without showering. The flickering of the bus stop lights makes his eyes look like lightning flashes within them. He's wearing a camouflage jacket that hangs loosely from his shoulders and is closed tight against the night air.

I remember him getting hit in the shoulder by Mary's bullet, but he does not seem to be favoring the arm. An armored vest?

"Steve," he says. "So nice to see you again."

"Max," I say.

For a moment, I contemplate the possibility of getting my hands on him before he can pull that trigger, and decide the odds aren't at all in my favor. I'd survive the blast, of course, but it would hurt like hell, and would take a couple weeks to recover from, if not longer. And I don't have any desire to be resting for a couple weeks while Division Six continues to search for me.

"You going somewhere?" Max asks.

"I'm leaving town."

"Looked like you were waiting for a bus," he says. "But that bus wasn't leaving town."

"It wasn't. I had thought to look for you, first."

The lightning flashes in his eyes are starting to bother me. I wish we could switch places.

"You were going to look for me? Why?"

"I have some questions I want to ask you," I say.

He snorts. "Questions. I could give you some answers."

"Why are you trying to kill me?" I ask.

"I'm not going to kill you," he says.

"But you shot at me."

He smiles, but his smile is lopsided and he doesn't expose any teeth. Then, something seems to click in his head, and his smile falters, giving me the impression that he's not quite all there.

"I can't let Division Six take you," he says. "You should have let me in."

"They told me someone was trying to kill me and was killing others like me."

Max looks around, past me, then at the street.

"Walk with me, back to George's place," he says.

He knows George's name. Of course he does. How else did he find me?

He slips over to my right, turns around, plants the gun in my side, and we start walking.

"Now, what you've got to understand is that Division Six will tell you anything to bring you into their program. They're collecting people like you, and they're trying to reverse some of the side-effects."

"Side-effects?"

Max nods, as if I understand what he means.

"When they get you, they'll inject their *cure* into you, and you'll be stuck taking it forever."

"Like Taggart?" I ask.

"Like Taggart," he says. "Though, he has it worse than the others."

"Worse?"

I'm having trouble following Max's story. He's trying to tell me something, but he's leaving out all the details as if they're unimportant.

"He hasn't run away, yet," Max says.

I try to remember what Taggart said about the drug. And as I think back, I remember the things he said it does for him, the less painful light, for instance, but I cannot remember that he said anything about side effects. And then I remember what he did say.

"He told me he can't leave," I say.

"Exactly," Max says.

"Why?"

"You can't figure it out?"

I want to hit him.

"Please," I say, instead.

There is a turn ahead that will leave us only one more turn from George's house. The leaves of a large fir tree overhang the corner, partially obscuring the streetlight.

"He can't leave because if he did, he would die."

I thought it would be something like that.

"That's not such a bad thing, is it? I mean, he's not susceptible to the light any more."

"True. He's not. But it is a form of slavery, and if he doesn't do what they want, they won't give him the drug." He pauses. "There's one other reason."

Somehow, I know what is coming if I ask the question he's leading me to, but I ask it anyway.

"What's the reason?"

"They made him the way he is," Max says in a sing-song voice, just like he used outside of Mary's apartment.

"What do you mean?" It is a dumb question. I know it. I know the answer, but I want to hear him say it, on the off chance that I'm wrong.

"They caused him to change, just like they caused you to change."

My breath catches in my throat, despite having guessed the answer. I suppose I had been hoping it was something else.

We reach the corner and turn down the street to the right. One more turn and we'll be looking at George's house.

"Why would the government do that to me?" I ask.

He laughs and pokes me with the gun in my side.

He takes a deep breath, a hint that he's going to use that sing-song voice again. "You're too funny. Division Six is not the government. They're a division of Archon Global Corporation."

The international conglomerate. Makers of weapons, food, chemicals, drugs, and who knows what else. Leaving the country isn't likely to put me outside their reach.

"The question remains," I say. "Why?"

"Project for the government, some other sort of drug trial, I don't know."

"You worked for them," I say.

"Where are you planning to go?" he asks, changing the subject.

"Somewhere else. I haven't decided." Playing coy seems the only option.

"That will hide you for a while, but they'll find you."

"They won't find me." But I need to do some better research—see if I can find out more about Archon and Division Six.

He pulls me into a shrub off the sidewalk just as a car turns the corner behind us. It's as if he heard the car before I did.

"They won't?" he asks as the car drives past us, its black exterior reflecting the streetlights, hiding the passengers inside.

We watch as it reaches the next corner and makes the turn. I know where it's going to stop—right in front of George's house.

CHAPTER 18

I try to run after the car, but Max holds me back, shoves the barrel of the gun hard against my ribs.

"What do you think you're doing? You don't want me to shoot you, do you?"

Another black car rolls by as I ponder how to answer his question. Him shooting me in the side wouldn't kill me, but it would hurt like hell. Besides, he's right. I know it. I can't do anything for them, right now.

"I need to save Mary," I say, weakly.

"Not now," he says.

"Taggart," I say, growing angry as I realize what I'm about to say. "Taggart led them to us."

"Possible, but I don't think he would do it on purpose."

"Why not? He works for them."

Of course, the answer is obvious, but in my fear for Mary and George, I can't see it.

"He saved you back in the tunnel," Max says.

Like I said. Obvious. If he did lead them to me, it wasn't on purpose. And, I realize as my rational mind starts to take back its control, it's been far too long since Taggart left George's house. If they had followed Taggart, they would have been there in minutes.

And then the implications of what Max said seep in.

"How do you know he saved me?" I ask.

"Guess."

"You were there," I say.

"Good guess, but wrong."

"Then how?"

"We have a . . . relationship."

What marbles I have left in my head have just shattered.

"That's not what it sounded like when I asked him about you," I say.

We watch another car roll by, black as the others. I'm getting tired of the gun in my side.

"Oh?" Max asks.

I think back to the words Taggart used. "He sounded almost like he has a grudge against you. He didn't seem to want to talk about you at all."

"Ah. He doesn't like me very much, but I can assure you, we are working together."

"Why doesn't he like you?" I ask, going for the easy question. The harder question, what he and Taggart are trying to accomplish, scares me.

A fourth car zooms past and squeals its tires as it takes the corner. I certainly can't help them now. Division Six will be there all night. They'll be searching the area, too, in a matter of minutes—if they haven't already started.

"We must leave," Max says, ignoring my question.

"No," I say. While I do not think I can help them, something in me won't let me abandon them.

"If you wish to live," he says, nudging my side with the gun, "then you will leave."

Thoughts of Mary in the hands of the Division Six people, on top of the stress of dealing with Max and his constant threat, spark my rage. I spin around, knocking his gun hand away with one hand, and put my other hand to Max's temple.

His eyes open wide in surprise, and I realize he is not as experienced at this as I thought. He can find me, he can search me out, but when it comes to the actual killing, he's still an amateur.

And this amateur knows what I can do to him.

"Please," he says with a tremor in his voice.

"Drop the gun," I say.

He apparently knows how fast I can take his soul, or whatever it is I do. I hear a thud when the gun drops to the soft loam beneath the bushes we are hiding in.

I conjure up as many B-movie cop shows as I can remember. "Start talking," I say.

He trembles under my fingers, but his jaw is steady. He's searching for his courage and is finding some of it.

"What do you want to know?"

What do I want to know? I want to know everything, but now is not the time for it. I could take it from him, steal it all, but that won't help Mary and George. I might need Max if I have to rescue them, which means killing him for his knowledge is out of the question.

"What will they do to them?"

"Maybe nothing, if you're not there. They may sit there for a week, waiting for you, or they may be taken for interrogation."

"They won't kill them?"

"Doubtful," Max says. "They don't want the government looking into their actions. Killing people draws eyes."

"So I have time. I don't have to try to rescue them right away."

"Rescue them? You don't need to rescue them. Stay away from them. They'll be fine."

"How do you know?"

"I told you, I worked for them. I know what they do."

"Then tell me why they did this to me."

"I told you why."

My fingers flex on his temple, just enough that I can see the worry in his eyes.

"You evaded the question," I say.

"Look, I don't know why they picked you. That was thirty years ago."

"Then why wait thirty years to contact me? Why now, why not back then?"

The whole thing just confuses me. I can't make any sense of it.

"I can't tell you."

"What do you mean you can't tell me? I can take the knowledge."

"But you won't," he says. "You need me."

How does he know?

"What do I need you for?"

"Protection."

Unbelievable.

"You were trying to kill me. Why would you think I would believe you would help protect me?"

"I don't want to kill you," he says. "But I won't let them take you, either."

"Why," I say very slowly and quietly. "Why do you care so much whether they take me or not?"

Under my fingertips, his skin suddenly cools. Nervousness, perhaps.

"They don't deserve to have you," he says. His voice is calm, steady, and chilling, just like his skin. The sing-song is gone.

CHAPTER 19

The sounds of the city at night are far away for a change, as Max and I hide in these bushes, my fingers on his temple, supposedly in control of the situation. But after his last statement, I'm certain that Max has changed. He's not who he was just two minutes ago, and I'm no longer certain I am in control.

And I haven't got the slightest clue as to what just happened.

"What do you mean?" I ask.

Before I can stop him, perplexed as I am at his sudden change, he punches me in the side and ducks his head away from my fingers. The blow is solid enough to knock me off balance, and I stumble backward a couple steps, out onto the sidewalk, and in plain view of anyone that might happen by, including Division Six agents.

The shadow is still pretty deep, and they might not see me, but I am suddenly in a far more vulnerable position than I was just moments ago.

He reaches for the gun where it still rests on the ground.

I launch myself into him, knocking him backward, away from the gun, and the two of us roll into the wet, dew covered grass of someone's front yard. He forces us to roll one more time, until he is on top of me, and he pins my arms with his hands. He can't do anything to hurt me this way, but I can do nothing to him, either. Stalemate.

His face is close enough, for the first time, that I can see the age lines in his face. There are scars, too. One down the right side of his face from his ear to his chin, another across his temple, but they look old, almost invisible.

He stares at me. His pupils are so dilated that his eyes are near black.

"They made you," he says, practically snarling. "But they don't know what they made. We are better than they realize, and they will rue the day they decided to try to contain us."

"Us? You're like me?" I ask, even more confused than before. I had thought he was a normal human, someone who had worked for Division Six, left, and was trying to do something to keep them from getting their hands on me. But now, I'm not so sure, and his strange behavior, from the sing-song voice to this darker side of him, has me just wanting to be free of him.

His weight and the position of my arms make it hard to fight back against him. I strain to move, but my arms go nowhere.

"Don't fight me," he says. "I am not like you any more. I am..."

A boot slams into Max's side out of the darkness, and he falls off me to my left, clutching at his ribs.

"Leave him alone, Max," says Taggart's voice. "We've got trouble."

A hand extends down from the dark. I take it, and the hand pulls me to my feet. I see Taggart standing there, the shroud of darkness over him like some thick blanket. He's trying not to be seen. The stench of another like me is a faint foulness in the air. My guess is that he's going to need another treatment soon.

"Trouble?" I ask.

"They've started searching for you. They'll be through here in a couple minutes."

"How did you find us?" Max asks.

I look back and see that he's retrieved his gun.

"I put a tracer on him," Taggart says, nodding in my direction.

"What the hell?" I ask.

"Now is not the time to discuss it," Taggart says. "You and Max need to leave, get out of town. I'll find you."

Sure, with the tracer. I'm going to find it and rid myself of it the first chance I get.

"What about George and Mary?" I ask.

"They'll be fine," Taggart says, but I find it hard to believe him. Something in his voice says to me that he thinks they're unimportant.

I look at Max. He still seems to be wearing the darker side of his personality.

"I'm not going with him," I say. "He's unstable."

"You must go with him," Taggart says. "Just don't ask him too many questions. What they did to him . . . he's one of us."

One of us.

Meaning someone like me, with the same abilities.

"But..."

"Look, he got a later version of the serum than I did. It mostly worked, but you're right, it left him a little unstable."

"I'm fine," Max growls.

"Just don't ask him too many questions," Taggart continues as if Max has said nothing at all.

"Can he do what I can do?" I ask.

"No. That's the part that left him unstable."

That's why he doesn't smell like one of us. He's not really one of us anymore.

"You're telling me they want to fix me, make me normal again?" I ask.

"No. They want to make you into something between Max and I—retain all your powers, without any of your disabilities."

"I don't see the problem," I say. Having my ability to protect myself, my ability to hide in the shadows, my ability to see in the dark, my ability to live practically forever, while gaining the ability to walk in the daylight and not give myself away to others like me? It sounds like a dream.

Max steps up close to me, puts his face right in mine so that I can see his scars again. "If they succeed, which there is no guarantee they will, your life will never be your own again. They'll never let you free, and there's always the chance that the government will stumble on this little project of theirs and shut it down. Taggart's stuck with them, and I'm a cripple. Do you want to be like us?"

It still sounds like a better situation than the one I've been in. I slip my hand into my pocket. My fingers brush against the clip for the Golden Eagle, just before they brush against my new passport, my new ID, my new life.

A dozen thoughts or more run through my head concurrently. Half of them are focused on the possibilities of my new life, others are focused on the difficulties I'll face in a new city, and yet, there is one that keeps pondering the possibilities of what Division Six might offer me.

I've been running on the advice of two men that I don't know, and who tell me to avoid something that offers a potential solution to the misery I've endured the last thirty years. They say they've saved me from their fate, but is that what they're doing? Or are they just trying to keep me stuck in my nightmare of a life?

A thrill and a shiver run through me as I come to a decision.

"No," I say. "I don't want to be like you at all."

"Good," Taggart says. "That settles it, then. You two need to move out…"

I break into a run, pushing my way past Taggart before his bulky arms can reach for me. Max chases after me, and I can feel him raising his gun to shoot.

If I were human still, my heart would be pounding in my chest, but it thuds along slow and steady as ever.

No shot arrives to strike me in the back. I'm free of them.

They must not know what I am doing.

But I know. Division Six doesn't have to be the enemy, do they? Maybe Joe was right. Maybe he didn't betray me at all. What if I've had it all wrong? What if Taggart is wrong and Max is really out to get me?

What if Division Six can fix me?

The allure of being normal is too much to withstand.

And in the pounding of my feet on the pavement, my aim taking me straight toward George's house and an unknown future, I'm certain I'm doing the right thing.

Aren't I?

At the very least, it'll save Mary and George, and that's just as important as anything right now.

CHAPTER 20

Four cars sit in front of George's house, not counting George's own vehicles. They are the same four cars I saw pass while I had Max's gun in my side, each of them black, and now, each of them empty.

Two men of similar height, though with very different builds, stand on the front porch. The one on the left is heavy, nearly to being obese, and the other is thin to the point of ridiculousness. The nursery rhyme about Jack Sprat and his wife comes to mind.

I don't see any others. Taggart said they had spread out to search for me, but I haven't seen any of them. If they did spread out to search, they went the wrong way.

I hug the shadows as I approach the house. In George's neighborhood, there are quite a few trees, and it's easy to flit from one to the other without being seen. I want to get close enough that it will be easy to jump them should I find it necessary. Walking up in plain view might be safer, but it's hard to trust anyone right now.

I manage to make my way to the side of George's attached garage. It seems like I did this at Joe's house only a few days ago.

I rest for a few moments and take some deep breaths.

While I rest, I slip the clip into the Golden Eagle. It seems safer than not doing it. If they're going to shoot at me, at least I'll have a chance to shoot back. But they won't shoot. They want me alive. Still, I slip the gun into my right-hand coat pocket. I know I should probably have it out, behind my back or something, but I don't want to provoke them.

Another deep breath helps only a little bit.

I want to do this.

Right?

Here I go, out in front of the garage, in between the garage door and the front of George's ancient black Impala. Jack Sprat and his wife can't see me yet.

I keep my right hand on the Golden Eagle in my pocket. I'll probably end up shooting myself if it comes down to a shootout.

I step out in front of them.

"Excuse me," I say. "Are you friends of George?"

The two of them look startled. The fat one stands still as a stone for three solid seconds. The second one backs away from me, fear plainly on his face, until the front door blocks any further passage into the house.

"S... Stay where you are," he says. So far, he hasn't pulled out a gun. I'm happy to see that after the shootout at Joe's.

"They probably should have given you a tranquilizer gun," I say. Not exactly calculated to put him at ease, but I'm nervous.

Jack Sprat's hand fumbles at the doorknob, but it won't open.

And then his wife breaks his silence with a bellow as loud as any I've ever heard come out of a human mouth.

"Miss Tanaka! He's out here!"

And then he jumps toward me like a flying boulder, or perhaps a giant gooey jelly-roll.

I stumble back, trying to get out of his way, but my heel catches on the edge of the walkway and I fall backward. My head cracks against a stone. Simultaneously, a monstrous weight lands on me and I hear an ear-shattering explosion.

My head disgorges a river of pain, and I can barely breathe.

My side seems to be getting wet, warm and wet.

Between the pain in my head and an inability to breathe, I quickly lose track of time and place until the world is just a dark blur that smells vaguely of hamburger and blood and garden mulch.

CHAPTER 21

Over the years of working with Joe, we learned a few things about my new existence. While most of my body is virtually indestructible, my head isn't. Hit me in the head with just about anything, and I can get woozy, or even black out with the best of them.

It doesn't last long, but the effect exists. One of my few weaknesses, I guess. I'm still better off in that department than a normal human would be. I still only get hurt by most things that will kill them. That's why Max carries that big knife with him. The gun to knock me out, the blade to finish me, or any others like me. And no, a single bullet to the brain won't do the trick unless it's a really big bullet. Two or three, though, work just as well as big.

It hasn't happened to me, but I saw another of my unfortunate ilk take one to the head, and he lived. He wasn't quite the same, after, but it didn't kill him.

So when I wake up in George's living room, I am not surprised. I doubt it has been more than five minutes. My hands are trapped behind me by cold steel handcuffs on my wrists.

A woman, Japanese from the looks of her, stands in front of me, hands on her hips, putting wrinkles in a finely cut black suit coat similar to the ones worn by all the Division Six goons. She's wearing slacks, too. She wears her hair cut short, just above her shoulders. I can't tell if she has any lipstick on. Her only real concession to femininity, and this is possibly debatable, are a pair of two inch long pearl earrings.

There are two other men in the room with her, both dressed like Division Six flunkies. One has a gun in his hand, but it looks to be one of the dart guns. The other has a hand up to his ear, and it appears he's listening to something in an earpiece. The curled wire that leads down the side of his neck is barely visible behind his wrist. The two of them are obviously subordinate to the woman.

I half expect to see Joe with them. If he came along, then he's somewhere else in the house, because he's not in the room.

"I see you are back with us," the woman says. It's the same voice that I heard at Joe's house, and it's all business.

I'm still barely processing anything except her, and can only acknowledge with a grunt.

"You didn't have to shoot Wendell," she says.

I remember the wetness, the warmth on my side. I look down and notice for the first time that I am not wearing the coat. There are some spots of red on my shirt where the blood soaked through the coat, but I am unharmed.

"He jumped me," I say.

"I know," she says. "Arny informed me that you didn't

actually draw the gun, but still it would have been better for all of us if you hadn't shot him."

Better for Wendell, for certain.

"It was an accident."

"I understand," she says. "Wendell shouldn't have jumped you in the first place."

She seems to be placing the blame on Wendell, which is fine by me.

Out of the recesses of my mind, the memory of the overlarge man leaping at me surfaces, and for the first time I remember what he had shouted.

"Miss Tanaka?" I ask.

"That's right. You remember Wendell's shout, then."

I nod.

"Good."

She glances around the room, then looks down on me again.

"Now this is no way to have this conversation. You likely feel you are about to be interrogated. Me, my feet hurt from standing. I'd like to talk with you about your future, Mr. Schrader, and I'd like to do it as comfortably as possible, but first, I need to be sure that you are not a danger to me or my men. Are you a danger, Mr. Schrader?"

"It's Steve," I say, "and no, I'm not a danger."

"You had the gun," she says.

"For protection. Joe told me someone was trying to kill me, so I picked up the gun."

"Joe," she says in a quiet voice, sounding like she's making a mental note. It isn't meant for me to hear, but as close to me as she is, the only way I could not hear what she says would be if she didn't say it at all.

"What?" I ask, pretending not to have heard clearly.

Someone knocks at the front door, and then it opens without an invitation. Taggart steps in, seemingly out of breath as if he had run a long distance, but it must be an act. Taggart is still my kind, and my kind doesn't get out of breath, as far as I know. I certainly don't. But maybe it's a side-effect of the drugs they have him on.

He looks at me, and then says, "You found him."

"He found us," Miss Tanaka says. "Didn't you Mr. Schrader."

Taggart's eyes widen, and this time, it's not an act. He did not expect me to come here of my own accord.

Then his eyes narrow as he realizes what it might mean.

I have leverage over him.

It occurs to me that it might upset Taggart if I told him his reaction had informed me of my leverage over him.

I don't have time to follow through on that idea, because Miss Tanaka continues to speak.

"What I want to know, Taggart, is what you've been up to. You have been out the entire night and have not reported in until just this moment, and you report in, here."

"I... I was on my way, ma'am," Taggart says. "I found him, and went to report in, but you were already out."

"You could have used your radio."

"I had a run in with Max," he says, casting a warning glance at me. "The radio got lost in the encounter."

Miss Tanaka's features turn to stone.

"Lost? After that stunt you pulled in the tunnel last week? You find Steve here, don't radio it in, then encounter Max and fail to radio that in as well? I thought you wanted to continue to receive the therapy."

Taggart shrinks into himself, as if afraid of a blow—a feat for a man of his size.

"I do," he says.

"You aren't acting like it." Her voice is cold steel. "If I didn't know better, I'd say you have a purpose in doing these things, that you are conspiring against me. You aren't doing anything of the sort, are you?"

"No, ma'am."

He looks over at me again, a warning, I'm sure, but I stare back blandly as if I don't understand what he's trying to imply.

Miss Tanaka turns slightly toward her man with the earpiece. He's still listening as she starts to turn, but when her eyes are looking at him, all of his attention shifts to her. "Braylon, take our wayward Minder here out to where he met Max. I want that radio back, and I want to see if you can track Max down."

She turns back to Taggart.

"Lucky for you, he didn't get this one," she says.

She means me.

She turns away from them, dismissing them. As I watch, her features lose the rigidity they had. I can almost see her stuffing her anger back in the box from which it had come.

"Now," she says. "Shall we have that conversation?"

CHAPTER 22

Miss Tanaka and I sit across George's dining room table from each other, a cup of coffee in front of each of us. I'm not going to drink mine, but it seems she needs the caffeine. I wonder how long it's been since she slept.

My wrists have been free for a few minutes, and I rub at them absently. The cuffs weren't on long, but it was long enough to make me very happy that Miss Tanaka had them removed.

"So," she says, but I interrupt her.

I haven't seen, or heard, from Mary and George. I should have asked about them earlier, but after knocking my head, and then the interesting interruption that Taggart provided, I forgot. But thinking about the coffee on George's table reminded me.

"Where are my friends?" I ask.

"They are safe, upstairs."

"I want to see them," I say.

"After we finish our talk. Trust me, they are safe."

Trust her. Right. I'm still not sure I can trust anyone.

I put my hands up on the table and surround the steaming cup of coffee with them. The cup is hot, but it feels good against my hands.

"Then talk."

"I work for Archon Global. I'm sure you've heard of us?"

"I have," I say. "You make all sorts of things from chemicals to weapons to toasters."

"Yes, though we also have quite a few other products, including pharmaceuticals, locomotives, and entertainment products, but what concerns us here are the pharmaceuticals."

Makes sense, given what Max told me.

"About fifty years ago, give or take, a small pharmaceutical company called the Tendike Corporation created a drug they hoped would bring about certain abilities in us that they deemed to be latent abilities. Things like telekinesis and telepathy, for instance.

"They managed to keep it secret for quite a long time, long enough to get close to running human trials. Then, Archon founder Brad Archon got wind of the drug and had to have it for himself. He bought Tendike Corporation before the human trials started, so he thought. He wanted to be among the first of the human trials."

"No doubt," I say, "because he wanted those abilities to help him grow his empire."

She lifts her cup of coffee to her lips, sips at it, then sets it down before answering.

"I am not certain of his motives, but the drug had a few problems. First, it turned out that it could only be administered to a fetus in the womb. The scientists at Tendike knew this, but they neglected to disclose that fact before the sale."

I'm somewhat surprised that Archon didn't ask about it, but I'm not about to ridicule her company's founder about his business acumen. Not in front of her, at least.

"What happened if it was given to an adult?"

"Insanity and death," she says.

"Were there other problems?" I ask, thinking that insanity and death were big problems.

"Yes," she says, "but you know about most of them."

I sit back in my chair and my hands come away from the warmth of the coffee cup. A shiver runs down my spine.

"I thought you said it didn't go to human trials," I say.

"No, that's the other piece Tendike neglected to mention before the sale. They had already taken it to a limited human trial at a pair of local hospitals. But when the children failed to develop any abilities after the first three years, they ran into difficulties."

"Funding."

"Yes. They had to sell, but they explained the financial issues away as unexpected development costs."

"So the drug didn't work?" I ask.

"It worked. Twenty or so years later, it worked. The abilities, and the side-effects, did not show themselves until adulthood."

"The change."

"Yes, I think that's what Joe said you called it."

So Max was only partially correct in putting the blame on Archon Global, assuming Miss Tanaka was telling me the truth. It could be corporate fiction, but it feels right, or at least close.

We sit for a moment, watching the steam rise from my untouched coffee, before I ask the question she expects me to ask.

"So you think I'm one of those early test babies."

"We know you are," she says. "We have the records to prove it."

"I want to see them," I say. I don't want to see them because I don't believe I'm one of them. I just want to see them as a way to prove her story.

"You will, when we are back at the lab."

"Assuming what you say is true, why wait thirty years?" I ask. "Why not contact me earlier?"

"We had contact with you through Joe."

Right. How could I forget.

"Why didn't Joe tell me what he knew?"

"What good would it have done? We didn't even have a division devoted to the drug at the time the change occurred. It had been shut down as a failure after Brad Archon's death. We didn't know about the trials, even, until years later when they came out during the investigation into his death. Records had been destroyed, executives sacked. By the time we had a list of the test subjects, the metamorphosis had taken place and every one of you had disappeared."

"But Joe?"

"Joe didn't work for Archon Global when he started working with you. We contacted him after AG formed Division Six in an effort to track down the test subjects and find out what happened to them. He had been making inquiries in various circles that got back to us and led the Division Six director at the time to find out if he did indeed have contact with you. At that time, they put him on the payroll and it was decided that you were to be kept in the dark for liability reasons."

"That sounds suspiciously like cover-your-ass," I say.

"Yes."

"Why not just kill me, then?"

"And lose a potentially huge resource of information on the drug that Tendike created and Archon Global now owned? Don't be silly. If the drug could be perfected, imagine the potential benefits for society." Her eyes fairly gleam as she speaks. She believes this.

"Imagine the profits," I say.

Her eyes narrow. "Those were a consideration."

A consideration. I may have been living on the streets for the last thirty years, but I'm not stupid. The benefits to society were likely never considered at the top of Archon Global, only the benefit to themselves and their shareholders.

"So why now?" I ask. "Why come for me now? Why use that gas on me in the tunnels? Why try to tranquilize me at Joe's house? Why not just have Joe talk to me?"

She spins her cup in place on the table, bringing my attention to her fingernails which are painted a deep, dark red. They stand out from the corporate image she projects.

"It's protocol," she says.

"I don't understand."

"We have tried to bring in others, and more than a few of those resulted in injuries to our employees."

"Deaths?" I ask.

"Some of those, too. Not all of the test subjects are as stable as you are."

"That's not surprising," I say. "I don't think I would be stable at all if it weren't for Joe's working with me. I was a real mess the first few years."

I still am, probably, but I had come to terms with my new existence, for the most part. I had thought I had come to terms with it, but after the events of the past few days, I'm starting to wonder.

"And the reason we came for you now," she says, "is that we think we have a way to fix your side-effects."

"Like Taggart?" I ask. The question slips out before I can restrain it.

Her eyes open wider than I have seen them. I have surprised her with the question.

"What do you know about Taggart," she asks, her tone much sharper than it has been to this point.

"I ran into him in the sewer," I say. I want to avoid mentioning that we had a conversation. "Something about him told me he was like me, but I couldn't smell him."

"The pheromones," she says. "Did he say anything?"

I don't know how to answer the question truthfully without getting him in trouble.

"Not that I recall. I saw him, and I ran."

"Why?" she asks.

"Something wasn't right about him," I say.

Her lips thin out into a slight frown that exposes a few stress lines that I hadn't noticed before.

"He has been a challenge," she says, her tone softening a little, "but no. You would not become like Taggart."

I wait, hoping she will elaborate, but silence stretches out between us.

"What would I become like?" I ask, finally, prompting her.

"You would lose your need to avoid the daytime, for one. You'd also lose the pheromones that announce you to others of your kind."

"What else?"

"Nothing else. You'd still retain what abilities you have. You'd still be practically indestructible."

It sounds too good to be true, and even though I don't really trust Taggart and Max, their words still make me cautious.

"Why? Why do this for me?"

"It's the right thing to do," she says. "You were wronged, and you deserve to be able to live among people again."

"That sounds like a corporate cover story," I say. It sounds like bullshit.

"It's the truth," she says.

"Not all of it. A conglomerate like Archon Global doesn't do things because they are right." Thirty years of seeing the underside of the city has ruined any fantasies I have had that people do things for the right reasons. They do them because they get something out of it.

"Of course not," she says, surprisingly. "But there are several reasons why I can't divulge what's in it for us, and even acknowledging that we're getting something out of it could put me in a bind with my boss."

"So what is it?" I ask. "What are you getting?"

"I can't say."

"Why?"

"I wish I could tell you, but I can't."

I don't have to work very hard to come up with reasons she doesn't want to tell me, and none of them are to my benefit.

"Maybe Max was right," I say.

"Max?" she asks, as if she doesn't know who I am talking about. But she talked about Max with Taggart less than an hour ago.

"Yes, Max Hall."

"Who is Max Hall?" The perplexed look on her face looks natural, but it has to be fake. She has to know I heard that conversation with Taggart.

"You were just talking to Taggart about him. He told me he used to work for you. He said..." I cut myself off. Just because Max said it didn't make it the truth. In fact, with the way his personality utterly changed on me, I'm not inclined to believe a thing he said.

"He said what?"

"He said you had tried to help him like you are going to help me." But he didn't say it. Taggart had said it. What game is Taggart playing? "He said you tried and failed."

She looks thoughtful, her mouth slightly open, her dark pink tongue just sticking out past her teeth.

"He claims to have been like you?" she asks.

"Yes. Joe told me that there was some guy that was hunting and killing people like me. When Max came to Mary's door just before you all showed up there..."

"Wait," she interrupts. "Max came to Mary's apartment? He knew where you were before we did?"

"Yeah, he told me he was there to save me from you."

"And then?"

"And then your men showed up, and he started trying to kill me, so I thought he was the one that Joe was talking about."

"When did he tell you he worked for us?"

"That wasn't until..." I stop, just before I say 'tonight'. I don't want to let her know I was with Taggart and Max.

"Until when?"

"Until a couple days ago." Until she wouldn't tell me what was in it for Archon Global to be helping me, I had started to trust her. But that refusal makes me unwilling to trust anyone anymore. And that is exactly why I feel like I must protect Max and Taggart to some degree. Maybe they were lying, maybe they weren't. Maybe they are just deluded.

"He didn't kill you then," she says, stating the obvious.

"No. We talked, I told him I was leaving the area, and he let me go."

"We saw your new identity."

"Tell me, do you know who Max is?" I ask.

"He was a patient, once. He . . . left."

"Why did he leave?"

"The treatment did not work well for him."

Apparently.

"What happened?"

"It was a different treatment, years ago," she says. "It has little relation to our new treatments."

She is trying to avoid telling me anything, and I'm regretting my return to the house.

"What was I thinking?" I ask.

"What do you mean?" Her pulse increases. I can see the vein in her neck thumping.

"I was leaving. I should have left. I shouldn't have come back here. You are just like Max said you were."

I stand up.

"Wait, we can help you."

"Then why won't you let me see Mary and George? Why won't you tell me what Archon Global gets out of the deal? Why won't you tell me what I'm really signing up for?"

"Sit," she says. The vein in her neck is really thumping now. I can smell the fear on her, but it's not fear of me. "I'll have your friends brought out here, and I promise, I'll tell you what I can."

"I want to see Joe, too."

"Fine," she says. "Just sit down again. It will take Joe a while to get here."

"How long?"

"It could be after the sun comes up."

I look at the curtains. They're all wide open.

"Close the curtains, and I'll wait," I say as I sit down.

Miss Tanaka's finger twitches, and I hear the pfft, pfft from a pair of tranquilizer guns before I have a chance to turn around. The darts each take a bite out of my neck, and the tranquilizer surges through my body.

Miss Tanaka stands over me as my vision starts to blur.

"It would have been easier if you had just said yes."

CHAPTER 23

The lights above me are bright when I wake up, the stark white alive with that almost imperceptible flicker of industrial fluorescent lighting. I try to cover my eyes with my arm, but my arm won't move. The strap holding me down isn't tight, but it's there, and I can't break free of it. A strap holds my other arm, as well.

I can move my head, however, and I turn it to the side, resorting to shutting my eyes against the glare. I still see the red-orange color of the inside of my eyelids.

While I wait for my eyes to adjust to the light, the memories of the last moments at the table with Miss Tanaka course through my brain.

I was stupid.

I know that, as surely as I know that I am at some Archon Global lab run by Division Six and Miss Tanaka. She wanted me to come peacefully, and I would have if she hadn't been so concerned with hiding her secrets. If she had let me see Mary and George, I would have gone along without very many questions. Being free to walk in daylight again is enough of an incentive to ask very few questions.

But now, all I want is to get my hands on Miss Tanaka and find out what she really knows. I have denied myself the use of my ability for so long, that even the thought of doing it again excites me. She'd be dead, and I'd have some remorse over that, but I have no illusions anymore that her motives are altruistic.

Before I open my eyes again, I resolve not to be stupid again. The lure of being *cured* is there, but if Archon Global feels like they have to kidnap me, the price may just be too high. As psychotic as Max may be, and as conflicted as Taggart obviously is, I can only conclude that they may have been right.

I start to open my eyes, slow as to help my eyes adjust to the bright light.

The room, as it becomes revealed to me, is as sterile as I suspect. White walls, no furnishings that I can see, and a door with a typical silverish door handle that you see in office buildings.

I turn my head to examine the other side of the room, and it's more of the same. The room appears to be without a window, for which I am grateful. No accidental sun exposure.

I look down my torso and see I've got a hospital gown on. My feet are bare. I try to lift a leg and find it's shackled, too. Both of them are.

I set my head back down and stare at the ceiling, wishing that this were some sort of nightmare, but I know it's not. It's far too real to be a dream.

The door handle jiggles, and I look to see who is going to enter. I hope it's Miss Tanaka. Briefly, I entertain the fantasy of breaking free of my restraints, placing my hands on her head, and taking everything she is from her, but when the door opens, it's not her at all.

It's Joe.

His balding head looks like he hasn't washed it in days, dark shadows haunt his eyes, and his shoulders wear the slump of an exhausted man. A white lab coat is draped over those shoulders and one of the many plaid shirts he always wears.

"What are you doing here?" I ask, instead of the obvious question. Where I am doesn't matter quite so much as why Joe came to see me, and what happens next.

"Anna Tanaka said you wished to see me," Joe says as he steps into the room and shuts the door behind him.

Now I have her first name, but I don't care about that for the moment.

"That was before," I say. "Now I'm not sure I have anything to say to you."

"As you wish," he says. "While I understand why you knocked me out back in my garage, I'm not feeling entirely partial to you, either."

Joe pulls a penlight from his lab coat pocket and steps toward the bed.

He reaches out with his free hand and plants it on my forehead, then tries to push my head so that it will face straight up. I resist.

"Do you mind?" he asks. "I need to check your vision."

"Of course I mind," I say. "You betrayed me. I know it was years ago, but you could have told me."

"Didn't we have this conversation in the garage?" he asks. "I am sorry you feel betrayed, but they found me, and they paid me for my findings. It was an opportunity I could not pass up, especially once they explained how they were trying to find a cure."

"A cure? You think they're really looking for a cure? Why do you think they kidnapped me and brought me here?"

Joe pauses for a moment, and stares off into space. Then his thoughts break loose and he returns to his attempts at straightening my head out.

"It was for your own safety," he says. "Your disease had progressed to the point that we could not trust you to not hurt yourself."

"What?" I ask, incredulous. "I haven't had a suicidal thought in years, Joe. You know that. I've been..." The word happy doesn't seem quite right. "I've been content, I was content until these people showed up. Why did it have to change, Joe?"

"I told you back at the garage." He pushes on my head with more force, and this time I let him. He has the light shining into my eye before I can take another breath.

The beam from the penlight bores into my skull. It doesn't hurt as much as I expected. It's just bright. Perhaps a special light designed specifically for people with my issues.

"You mean Max," I say.

The light falters for a moment.

"Max? I don't know who you're talking about."

"Don't lie to me, Joe. You know. Don't act like Miss Tanaka. You and I were friends for twenty years. You can tell me."

"Yes," he says. "I mean Max."

He moves the light to my other eye. Again, it's bright, but not painful like I expect.

"Did you know he didn't show up to try to take me out until after your friends tried to grab me?"

"Yes." He pulls the light from my eye. "The eyes look good."

"What do you mean?"

"I mean you don't have any obvious damage to them."

A hardly enlightening statement.

"Is anyone ever going to tell me what's really going on?" I ask.

"I was led to understand that Anna filled you in," he says.

He backs away from the table, as if he's about to leave.

"Why are you doing this, Joe? Doesn't the time..."

"Look," he says, and focuses on me for the first time since he entered the room. "It's cutting edge science, Steve, and they're paying me a lot of money. I enjoyed most of the time we spent together, and this is the culmination of that time. It really is for your own good. After this is over, you should have all of your abilities without any of the drawbacks. Don't you want that?"

"I do," I say, "but she won't tell me what Archon is going to do after they fix me. Why do they even want to fix me, Joe? What are they hoping to learn? How are they making money from this? I can see how making the original formula work would be useful, but fixing us? What's the point of fixing us when we're the only group that needs fixing?"

Joe opens his mouth to say something, then shuts it. I've stumped him. He clearly hasn't thought about it. Mr. Science had thought only about the science, and not about the reasons.

"I'm your friend, Joe, aren't I? Yet I'm here, strapped to this gurney because they say I'm a danger to myself, and you believe them. How can you believe them after all we've been through."

After a moment, he says, "They've only ever been interested in your well being."

I lift my arms against my restraints. "Does this *look* like they're interested in my well being? They're after something, Joe. I don't know what it is, but why would Max want to keep them from getting to me? Why would he kill me, and others, to prevent that from happening?"

"Because he's got a grudge against Archon, and he wants to shut the whole project down."

"Why does he have a grudge?"

I want to get off this table and strangle Joe, force him to understand. I can't remember the last time I was so frustrated.

"Because the attempt to cure him removed all his abilities," Joe says. "It also drove him partially insane."

"Insane enough to want to kill the rest of us just so that we don't get hurt like him? Is he jealous? I don't think that's it, Joe. It can't be it. I talked with him. He doesn't want me dead." Well, not most of the time.

I can see, though, that I'm not getting through to Joe. He believes in the science. He believes the motivations of Miss Tanaka and Archon Global are pure and altruistic, and because he's so invested in the science, he's not willing to question those beliefs. It's in his face, in the way his eyes don't really want to look at me, in the way his body is half turned to leave and is just waiting for the opportune moment.

"I have to go, Steve. I wish I could explain to you how lucky you are, how you'll be getting your life back, perhaps even better than before. I know you can't see it, but in less than six hours, I won't have to help you see it."

He turns away from me.

My next words are directed at his back.

"You're the one that's blind, Joe. You've let the science overcome your sense!"

He doesn't give any indication that he heard my words, and the door shuts behind him, leaving me to myself and the bright white lights.

CHAPTER 24

I had thought the lights in the room where they were holding me were bright, but they don't compare at all to the lights in the room I find myself in now. After I spent several hours contemplating my conversation with Joe, two men in white lab coats came into the room and wheeled me out, taking care to stay well away from my hands. Even as they wheeled me down a corridor, I could not stop pondering the one thing I still haven't figured out.

Why the hell did Joe look at my eyes, but not check any of the rest of me?

Now, I'm in the center of the room where they left me, surrounded by several computers and those big, moveable lights that you see in operating rooms. There is all sorts of other equipment, too, but none of it looks familiar to me. Not that I would know. I haven't seen the inside of a hospital in twenty-five years.

One table, covered with a cloth, looks a lot like a table used to hold medical tools during an operation. It appears to hold several long cylinders underneath the cloth. I can only imagine what they are, but if I understand what's about to happen to me, I'm probably not far off.

Several minutes pass while I wait for someone, anyone, to enter the room and tell me just what they're going to do to me. While I wait, I stare at that table and listen to the air conditioner run. I wonder what they've done with Mary and George.

Mary. I don't even know what to think any more. Even near fifty, she's still as attractive to me as ever, but she's had a separate life, a real life, and I've had nothing. She still wants to be with me.

Maybe, if this works, if Miss Tanaka is not lying to me, if Max is somehow wrong and I do get my life back, Mary and I can figure things out. She's stood by me all these years since her husband died, and I kept her at arms length because I'm not worth much of anything.

But if I'm cured?

Only, Max and Taggart seem to think I'll be just as trapped by Archon Global as Taggart is.

God, I hope Mary's all right. I hope they sent her home, left George alone, fed them some lie about how I was safe or ill or anything.

The door opens. Since my feet point toward the door, I have to lift my head to see who enters. Two men and a woman, all wearing lab coats. I don't recognize any of them. Following on their heels, Miss Tanaka enters, still dressed in her suit. I glance at her fingernails, and discover that she took the time to change their color to a dark violet that almost glows.

"I see you are awake, Mr. Schrader."

"I've been awake for hours."

"Yes, I know."

"Where are Mary and George?" I ask.

"Home safe. They are unimportant to us."

That's good, at least, assuming I can trust her. I can't, though.

She walks across the room, then steps near me, though safely out of reach of my hands.

It has been so long since I last used my ability, since I learned to control it, since I chose to stop harming people, that I almost feel guilty for thinking that if she stepped just close enough, I'd use it on her. But only almost. Right now, if I could put a hand on her, I would consume everything that makes her who she is. I would learn her secrets, and I don't think I would feel too bad at all.

She's not going to give me the chance, however.

"Now, Mr. Schrader, I thought I should let you know what's about to happen to you."

"You're going to cure me, you said."

"In a manner of speaking," she says. "We are going to cure you, but we are also going to recruit you. You will work for us, help us track down the rest of your kind so we can cure them, too."

"Why would I work for you?"

"Why? You won't have a choice," she says. "You see, the government knows about our little project, about the failures, but they also can see the potential military and espionage benefits. They want all of you under control before they will give us approval, and funding, for more testing of the Alpha Serum."

"Like Taggart?"

"Somewhat. He's flawed, however, and now that we have you, we no longer need his services."

She must have figured out his duplicity, or maybe she knew of it all along and dealt with it because she had little choice. I wonder what it means for him, though. I can't imagine they'll just fire him and continue to give him his injections.

The door opens again, and I get a glimpse of Joe as he enters the room.

Miss Tanaka takes that as her cue to end our discussion.

"Enough of the niceties. In a few moments, we will begin to administer the protocol that should remove your side-effects. Joe can answer any questions you might have about the procedure, but I suggest you relax and anticipate the new life that you are about to have. It only gets better from here, I promise."

She smiles for the first time that I can remember. It doesn't exactly light up her face, but instead reveals the predator like quality that I had already guessed lived within her.

"I'll see you when it's over," she says, then turns and leaves.

One of the technicians, as bland and unmemorable a face as I have ever seen, reaches across me, undoes the plastic snaps that have kept my hospital gown together, and pulls it down to bare my chest.

The other technician begins pulling those little electrodes out of one of the machines and lays them, one by one, across my body. He then reaches into a drawer, pulls out a pair of thin leather gloves, and puts them on. They're long enough that they cover any exposed skin on his wrists. I look at the first technician and see that he was wearing gloves, too, but I had missed them.

These guys have been told what I can do, and they're not taking any risks.

The tech starts attaching the leads to my chest. While he's doing that, the other tech wraps a restraint across my hips and ties additional restraints around my arms so that they are practically immobile.

"Are you ready for your new life?" Joe asks, startling me.

He pulls the cloth from the table, exposing a half dozen syringes and just as many glass containers, five of which look like they are filled with cloudy water, each of which is successively more cloudy. The sixth vial is clear.

"Not if you're putting that in me," I say. "Why are you doing this, Joe?"

"It'll be good for you," Joe says. "No more worry about going out in the daylight, no more having to live in the sewers and other dark places of the city. You'll have a job, can get your own place. It's all for the best."

"How can you be sure that what happened to Taggart and Max won't happen to me?" I ask.

Joe picks up the first syringe and plunges its needle into the rubber top of the least cloudy of the cloudy vials.

"Because I solved all of the problems, Steve. First, with Taggart, there was an issue with the serum that made his cells unstable if he didn't continue to receive additional doses. With Max, it took away his abilities, as well as the side-effects. The loss of his abilities unfortunately brought about some emotional issues that have perplexed us."

Joe draws out nearly all of the liquid in the vial, withdraws the syringe, and sets the vial back down on the tray.

"You solved the problems?"

"With your help," he says, and reaches out and pats me

on the shoulder, but on the last pat, he leaves his hand there for a second and squeezes before withdrawing it.

"My help?"

I look up at Joe's face, but I can't read it. I feel like he was trying to tell me something with that squeeze, but what? It's lost on me.

"Of course, with your help. I've been working all these years to cure you, and now, finally, here we are."

"I thought you were doing it on your own," I say.

"No one ever does anything like this on their own."

He lifts the syringe up so the air bubbles float to the top, then depresses the plunger just enough to squeeze out the air. When the air is out, he sets the syringe on the tray and picks up another bottle and a cotton swab.

Joe turns to the two technicians who are now busy watching the readouts on the screens.

"Are we ready?" Joe asks.

"Ready," says one of them. They don't turn their heads, so I can't tell who it is that spoke. Not that it matters. They're only here to watch the show, it seems.

Joe holds the cotton swab up against the opening of the bottle and pours whatever is in the bottle against the cotton. Alcohol, or... No. Iodine. I can smell it.

Joe takes hold of my right arm. He's wearing gloves, too, but only thin rubber gloves. He's worked with me long enough, knows how I had to struggle to control myself. He trusts that I won't hurt him. Or maybe he trusts the restraints. I couldn't reach him with my hands if I wanted to.

He swabs my arm with the iodine, then trades the iodine bottle and the swab for the syringe that will change me forever, again.

The needle on the syringe slips into my arm, and it burns going in.

"Here we go," Joe says.

He depresses the plunger on the syringe.

The sting of the needle is nothing compared to the fire that begins to course through my veins.

I scream. Not even the bullet I took for George hurt this much. I pull hard against the restraints, trying to move my arm away from the demon that has invaded my flesh. The restraints prevent it.

Then Joe removes the needle and the fire stops entering my body. What's still in it continues to burn, but it's slowly fading.

Joe is working on a second syringe while I writhe in pain on the table. He says something to the techs, and they grunt something back, but the actual words they say escape me.

Joe bends over me so that I can see his face.

"You okay, Steve?" he asks. His eyes are clear, I can see that much. I seem to see real concern in them, too, but if he's doing this to me, how can it be real?

"Only four more, and then it's over," he says. "We'll give this one a few minutes to take, you'll know it when the pain subsides, and then we start the next one. It's a bit like making mayonnaise. You pour in the oil, in this case, the serum, a little at a time at first, and then gradually increase the amount until it's all in.

The pain is already starting to fade, though not fast enough. It's being replaced by a strange feeling that is spreading throughout my body. I'd say it's a tickle, except that it doesn't tickle. I don't even know how to explain it. Perhaps more like an itch I can't scratch.

Joe looks at his watch, a slight, silver model which would look more appropriate on a woman. He glances toward the door, then back to his watch.

"Five minutes," he says. "Are you ready, Steve?"

I say nothing.

I don't have to. After a moment, one of the techs says, "He's ready."

I wonder how they know. Some chemical reaction they're monitoring in my body?

Joe swabs the area with iodine again, and then jabs me a second time.

This time, it's not fire, but an entire nuclear meltdown that enters me and eradicates every thought beyond wishing for it to end. It works through me like a wave, and where it passes, I can feel that things are different. The itch is still there, but more pronounced. I try to reach it, scratch it, but something holds my arms and I cannot do anything about it.

Once the meltdown is over, I find I can breathe again. The itch is still there, but it has become more bearable.

"What are you feeling, Steve?" Joe asks. His voice sounds different, somehow. I can hear reticence, worry, that wasn't there before. I know he is concerned about something.

Me? Has it gone wrong already?

"She said a little pain," I say. "It's like napalm in my veins."

"Still?" He sounds even more worried now.

"No. Now, I just itch everywhere."

"Okay, that's fine. That's expected."

He looks at his watch again, then back up to the door, as if he's expecting someone to walk through it at any moment.

"None of this is expected," I say. "I'll kill you when I get the chance."

His head turns sharply to look at me. For the first time, I notice he already has the next syringe ready.

"You don't mean that," he says.

I don't answer. Let him believe what he wants.

Then he whispers. "You don't mean that."

I don't really mean it. In spite of his betrayal, he helped me out of the mental gutter I was in so long ago. He never managed to get me out of the actual gutter, until perhaps, now. And if this works, I'll probably forgive him, though not too quickly.

"You shouldn't have lied to me," I say.

He glances at his watch. I'm not surprised he ignores me.

"Ready?" he asks.

He swabs my arm, and then reaches down underneath the tray and pulls out something that looks like a mouthpiece.

He holds it in front of my mouth and says, "You'll want this."

I open my mouth and slips the mouthpiece in. I bite down. After a couple minutes, I'm sure it will make me drool, but I don't think that's the worst of my problems. Joe uses my preoccupation with the mouthpiece to distract me while he stabs me with the third syringe and pushes that milky white pain cocktail into my arm.

I tense up, waiting for the pain, but it doesn't come. The needle hurts, of course, but I had expected something even more excruciating than the last time, though I can't imagine anything more excruciating.

I am about to spit out the mouthpiece and ask why there isn't any pain this time when my eyes catch fire and my brain explodes. My vision clouds over and I cannot see anything but a bright orange haze. My jaw clenches upon the mouthpiece. I couldn't spit it out if I wanted to. It's locked in place. I want to bring my hands up to my eyes so that I can dig out the fire, but the restraints hold them still.

The orange I can see changes, grows darker, then lighter, approaches white, then resolves into an image. I see myself as if I'm looking down on my body, strapped to the table, veins along my neck and at my temples standing out, pushing at the skin that contains them. I wonder briefly if I'm dying and I'm having an out of body experience.

But the image shifts and I'm looking at a computer screen. A line that looks like an electrocardiogram runs across the screen, the beat pulsing in time with my own heartbeat. Above it, there are other lines, one that looks like it's slowly descending, another that just seems to jiggle nonsensically, and a pile of numbers whose labels make no sense to me. Then it shifts again and I'm looking down on the room through a heating vent or grate or something. Joe is standing there, looking over me, watching, waiting, and I'm laying on the bed, muscles contracted. I cannot see the other two men in the room, though.

The pain subsides almost as quick as it came on, and the visions end. All I see now is the dark of my closed eyelids.

And I have enough control over my thoughts to wonder what it was that I just saw. The visions remind me of what I see when I first start to take someone, when I first start to steal their mind, only I wasn't touching anyone, and it was only like that first part. None of the history, none of the memories or the context came with it.

"How do you feel?" Joe asks as he takes the bit from my mouth.

"Odd," is all I can say.

The pain is gone, most of the tickling has subsided, but

there is something else there, mostly in my mind, pulling at the edges.

"Odd? How so?"

"I'm not sure. My head almost feels like I'm floating. I have the memory of the pain, but there's something else, indescribable."

Joe checks his watch, looks at the door, then up at the lights. His agitation is starting to agitate me. I would almost call him nervous, but it makes no sense that he would be nervous.

The two technicians continue watching their readouts. I try to get a glimpse at the screen closest to me. It is hard to see around the guy's head, but it looks like the same screen I saw in my vision—only then, it was much closer than I have ever been to it.

He turns to the table and picks up the next syringe and starts to fill it.

"Two more to go," he says quietly, talking to himself—too quiet for the other technicians to hear.

But there are three vials left. Two of the milky stuff, and the other one.

I don't question him. I'm still trying to figure out what those visions were about, and it's possible I just misheard him.

It's the same procedure with this one. Joe asks if I'm ready, the technicians say yes, he swabs me and injects me.

This time, the pain creeps over me slowly. It's not as intense as any of the previous injections, but the orange fog comes over me again.

And then the vision from above, in the air duct, only this time, with words.

It's almost time. One more, then boom.

No. Thoughts.

The vision shifts, and I'm looking at readouts again.

...what Joanne will come up with today? That hand...

The vision shifts a third time, and I'm looking down at myself. My eyes are wide open, but still.

...syringe to go. I hope they're right about...

A fourth shift. I sit behind a desk, staring out a window. There are fir trees across a parking lot, and they block the view beyond. The parking lot has several black cars in it that look suspiciously like Division Six cars. The view shifts down to look at a computer screen, and in the periphery, toward the bottom, I can see a pair of hands on a keyboard, lying there. The fingernails are painted a dark purple color.

...not much longer, now, and we'll know if Joe was right. God, I hate waiting for...

One last shift, and I'm back in my own head.

If Joe was right? Right about what?

And then the bigger thought hit me.

The nails. The purple painted nails. I saw them earlier on Miss Tanaka. That wasn't just a vision. I was in someone else's head, that bitch Tanaka's head.

I glance at Joe. He's in the right place. And the technician? I was in his head, too.

But then, what was that other view? I look up toward the ceiling. Was someone up there, watching? In secret?

I see a vent up there, but I can't see into it. The lights in the room are too bright, behind the vent, too dark. There are other vents, too. I check those, but I can't see anything.

"I need to get this last one in him," Joe says in a whisper that carries to my enhanced ears, but not to the technicians across the table. But wait, was that a whisper, or was it in his head? Was I listening in on his thoughts?

I look at him and he's already prepping the next syringe. It's not the last one, though. There's still one more after that. What the hell?

The fifth syringe is full with the last of the milky vials.

He glances at his watch. A drip of sweat rolls down his temple. It isn't hot in this room.

"Come on," he says. His lips move, so he's talking—not in his head, or mine.

Maybe it was all a hallucination.

"Is he ready?" he asks, but he's not asking me. He doesn't care what my answer is.

"The numbers are good," says the technician without turning around.

He swabs my arm in a hurry, then injects the fluid.

My back arches, my spine contracts, and the pain is worse than any of the others.

A loud bang echoes through the room, and everything goes dark. In my pain, I assume it's just another effect of the drug. I can hardly think.

Then there are flashes of light, accompanied by the sound of gunfire. Maybe I'm imagining it.

Shouts, incoherent, or I can't understand them.

Another flash and gunfire explosion, followed by a scream.

Someone backs into the table near my right hand. I feel flesh.

I need to stop the pain.

I lose control.

I squeeze.

CHAPTER 25

At first, I see black. The memories start the moment I make contact, they flow from my victim to me, usually from the most important to the least, until there is nothing left. But they almost always start with the moment of contact.

In a fraction of a second, I know it's Joe, but it is already too late to stop. Once I've started, I can do nothing but take it in, take his life from him and use it for myself.

And I take it.

I see myself laying on the table, just like I did minutes ago.

They better not be late, or all this is for nothing. I won't have a choice but to administer the binder, and then it will all be for naught, and Steve will truly hate me.

I don't have even a moment to digest the memory before another one comes.

I see a car, an eighties model Oldsmobile sedan, black. A man stands next to it

'You've already found him,' the man says. 'Let us help you do the work. We'll pay your expenses, put you back on the payroll. You'll have a career again. You can bring him in...' says the man.

'No, he won't come in. He's paranoid, thinks someone is after him. He flips from almost normal to delusional at the slightest provocation. I'll just keep going as I am,' Joe says.

And then, another memory, this one in an office. Joe sits in a chair across from Miss Tanaka.

'You think you can do it?' she asks.

'I know it will work this time. Do you need me to explain again where we went wrong?'

'No. I trust you. If it does work, you'll get your bonus.'

Joe leans forward.

'You swear he won't be harmed, after?'

'You have my word,' Miss Tanaka says.

Now, the memory is of standing in a hallway, apparently in the same building, and I hear voices.

'The CIA wants all materials, including the subject,' says Miss Tanaka's voice.

'You must be kidding,' says a man's voice I don't recognize.

'They can shut this down, all of it, and your father will never get his cure. Joe's serum is the best chance we've had, and we need to make it happen. The only way it happens is if the CIA gets what it wants. You may run this company, Ander, but..."

'Don't threaten me, Anna. I know what the CIA has over us. I know if this comes out, it will be the end of my father's company. Make sure it works. We'll give the CIA what they want after we get my father back.'

Now, Joe kneels in some dark place, staring down at a headless body, splayed out on wet, black asphalt that reflects a flickering flashlight.

'What happened?'

'He's dead,' says Taggart's voice.

'You were supposed to bring him in. How did he get dead?'

'I found him like this,' Taggart says. 'He was alive two days ago.'

'Cops?'

'They won't come down here of their own volition,' Taggart says.

'What am I supposed to tell Anna?'

'The truth?'

'She'll want to use Steve,' Joe says. 'I can't let that happen, yet.'

Joe starts to walk away, then turns back and sees Taggart standing over the body, one hand running through his rain dampened hair.

'Find another,' Joe says. 'I'll stall her somehow.'

Then a memory where Joe is staring out Miss Tanaka's window.

'They want super-spies,' Miss Tanaka says, 'and you're going to get that for me. You are going to make it work, or you will be in prison, this whole project shut down, and your friend will never see the outside of a laboratory again.'

'The trials weren't my fault,' Joe says.

'But you were the lead researcher, and you had a duty when Archon Global bought Tendike to tell us what had happened. I am surprised all they did was fire you, back then.'

'I had no control,' Joe says. 'They took it from me, despite my warnings...'

'We're not here to argue about the past,' Miss Tanaka says. 'We're discussing your future. Fix the protocol, get

Brad what he wants, give the CIA their super-spies, and I'll let you help your friend. I'll even see to it that you get enough of a bonus that you can live out the rest of your days in peace.'

More memories flood into my head, memories of Joe growing up, memories that were happier, memories of Joe at Tendike, all fogged by years and age.

And along with the memories, his life force, so much that my body tingles, alive with energy. I feel better than I have in three years, since the last time I slipped backward and allowed myself to take someone.

I had forgotten, but I know, now.

And when I release his hand, the remorse hits me, the pain of knowing that I've killed again, before his body even falls to the floor, before I understand the chaos around me.

CHAPTER 26

Another gunshot rings out, bringing me out of my initial dive through Joe's memories. The anguish in my chest over my murder of Joe will have to wait.

I'm in danger, the lights are out, the smell of gun smoke permeates the air.

And I'm strapped to this bed.

Suddenly, hands fumble in the dark at the straps holding me down.

"Steve, stay calm. Are you all right?"

It sounds like Max. My vision is still blurry from the drugs and the theft of Joe's life. I cannot see well in the dark, yet, but I know that will return.

"I'm fine," I say.

"What happened to Joe?"

"I don't know," I lie. I'm hardly ready to admit what happened to myself, I'm not going to spill it to Max. "What are you doing here?"

The first strap falls away.

"Saving your ass," he says as he goes to work on the strap near my wrist. "It looks like he didn't give you the binder, yet."

"The binder?" I remember something about that from Joe's memories, but I need time to sort them out.

"Joe told me it would work like Taggart's broken protocol. It would keep you from leaving Archon Global for any length of time."

The strap on my wrist loosens, and my right arm is free.

He reaches across me and works on the other straps.

"Hurry up, man," says a voice out of the dark, somewhere near the door. It sounds like Taggart.

"They strapped him down good," Max says.

I use my free arm to work at the other strap that keeps me down.

"Wait," I say. "Joe told you? He was working with you?"

"No time to wait," says Taggart. "Security is coming."

The straps on my arms fall away, and all that's left are the ones on my ankles. Max moves to them, and I rip off all the monitoring leads so that I can sit up and help him.

The straps on my ankles fall away, and I'm free.

I swing my legs off the table and try to stand, but I'm a little wobbly, dizzy. I have to catch myself on the table.

"We should have just wheeled him out of here," Taggart says.

"Then we'd just have to undo him in the parking lot," Max says.

"Can you walk?" Max asks me.

"I don't know," I say.

He comes over to me, slips an arm around my back, and helps to steady me.

"Joe said the drugs might make you dizzy for a bit. Why the hell did he have to go and get caught in the shooting. He was supposed to help us."

Max starts pushing me forward, and I walk as well as I can. I have to use one hand to hold up my hospital gown. It seems I have underwear on beneath it, but nothing else.

Taggart opens the door. The hallway is lit with orange-yellow emergency lights.

My eyesight is no longer quite so blurry, and I can see the handgun Taggart has in his right hand while he holds the door with his left.

Max hustles me through the doorway into the hallway. I hear the door shut behind me, and then Taggart slips past us and runs the length of the hallway to the airlock at the far end. I remember from the trip in that the corridor extends beyond it.

We go as fast as my wobbly legs allow. I can feel Max's impatience, but he's not letting it show, and his mouth stays shut.

"Why are you doing this?" I ask.

"Later," he says. I think I almost hear the other Max, the one that got angry at all my questions, the one that wanted to shoot me not too long ago.

Probably better to ask Taggart why.

About half way toward Taggart, I start to sense someone in the hallway beyond the airlock. I can feel them, feel their heartbeat, just like I realize I've been feeling Taggart and Max.

In my surprise, my left foot drags and I almost fall. Only Max's arm around my back keeps me from hitting the floor.

"Hey, stay with me," he says.

I get me feet under me.

"I'm fine I say. There's someone in an alcove down the corridor on the other side of the airlock."

"What?" he asks.

"Someone is there, waiting."

"Who?"

"I don't know," I say. But I do know. "Miss Tanaka."

"Shit," Max says. "You sure?"

"Yes," I say.

She just feels the same, just like from the vision I experienced after Joe injected me.

What did he do to me? I've been able to hear things better, smell people better, ever since the change, but this is something different. There's no way I can smell her or hear her through that airlock, but I know she's there. The answer must be somewhere in the memories I stole from Joe, but I need time to rest in order to sort through them. They're all just a jumble in my head.

We reach the airlock and Taggart opens it. We slip inside and wait for the air to cycle. I hear Max tell Taggart about Miss Tanaka, but I don't hear a response from Taggart. I'm just trying to stay upright. My legs feel like they are getting weaker, my head is swimming in memories and visions and whatever else Joe injected into me.

When the second door on the airlock opens, Max pushes me through the door, and I stumble and fall up against the wall.

I catch Taggart rushing past us again, but in that moment, what I see changes, and I'm looking around a corner down a hallway. A large shadow rushes toward me. It's Taggart, I know, but I'm seeing him from the front, not from the back like I should.

"Taggart!" It's Miss Tanaka's voice, both in my head and from down the hall. It has a slight echo to it. "What do you think you are doing?"

"Getting him out of here," Taggart says as he slides to a stop in front of me... Not me... Miss Tanaka. "We aren't lab rats, and we don't belong to the government."

"You're making a mistake," she says. "It'll be the end for you."

"I'm okay with that," he says as he reaches out for me, for her. "I'm not going to turn any more of us into slaves, and I'm not going to let you do it, either."

I feel the fear through the vision, Miss Tanaka's fear wells up within her. Taggart is large, strong. She knows he could break her neck. She knows what else he can do, that he can make her do whatever he wants if he touches her.

I feel my own body being carried down the hallway by Max.

"Don't do it," Miss Tanaka says.

"Don't do what?" Taggart asks.

I feel the pressure of his fingers on her skin as if it were my own.

My contact with her breaks, snapping me back into my own body.

I look up and I see we're just passing the alcove where she was hiding, where Taggart is now doing something to her. I can't tell if he's killing her, or making her do what he wants. I have no idea what he wants.

But she no longer makes any noise.

Max drags me along the corridor until I can get my feet under me. I am feeling a little less woozy and more in control of myself. If I can keep any more visions out of my head, I should be able to walk on my own, but I have no idea how to keep them from taking over.

It reminds me of the days after the *change* came over me, when I had these new abilities that I couldn't control. Things would just happen, and I'd have to pick up the pieces afterward. Too many people died before I could control it. Too many years passed before I found Joe.

Found Joe? Or did he find me?

I push that aside for another time. Getting out of this place has to be the first priority, finding Mary and George, second. After that, I'll figure out just what Joe did to me. Just in case these new abilities have some serious consequences that I can't control.

I don't want that to happen again.

And yet, I killed Joe.

I must stop thinking about it for now. I must.

My feet are under me, which is a start, but it's not enough. I need to separate myself from Max.

"I can walk," I say.

"You sure?"

"Yeah." I'm not sure, but I have to try. That was the problem back then. I let it all happen. I didn't even try to exert control at first.

Max looks at me skeptically, then slowly withdraws his arm and leaves me to stand on my own. He waits for a moment, ready to catch me, until I prove I can stand on my own.

After a wobble or three, I manage to prove it to him enough that he withdraws his hands completely and takes a step down the corridor.

Taggart runs past us, again.

"Let's go, they're waiting for us," he says.

They?

"Who's waiting for us?"

"The others," Max says, and then starts down the corridor after Taggart, though not so quickly as the big man.

I take my own first steps alone, tentative probing steps to make sure I can keep my balance despite my swimming head. I can. I speed up. I don't dare run, but I can go faster alone than Max was going when carrying me.

I risk a look behind. A shadow stares down the corridor after us, Miss Tanaka, by the silhouette.

The corridor ends at an elevator, and a passage off to the right leads, if the sign on the wall is to be believed, to a stairwell and the emergency exit.

Taggart heads toward the stairwell, and we follow him.

The movement is helping to clear my head of the wooziness. It keeps me focused on the moment instead of thinking about what might really be going on, why Joe was working with Taggart and Max, and what had happened to my abilities.

Again, Max and I precede Taggart through a doorway, only this time, Taggart stays behind us as we head down the stairs. The stairway is lit only a little better than the hallway was. My guess is that the people waiting for us are the ones that cut the power.

We descend down one flight of stairs, two.

"Why is there no one else in the stairway?" I ask, suddenly realizing that it seems very odd to have seen only Miss Tanaka in the building. There were doors along the hallway that presumably led to offices or other workspaces.

"There aren't too many people that work in this building, and it's after dark," Max says.

"Half the group is out tracking down another one of us," Taggart says as we turn a corner to head down another flight of stairs.

"They won't find him," Max says.

"Why not?"

"He's already dead," Max says, and laughs.

"You..."

"No, no," says Taggart. "This guy died about two years ago, and not because of us. The team doesn't know that, though."

"A ruse?" I ask.

"Yes," he says. "And Anna should keep them out in the field long enough for us to escape."

So that was what he had Miss Tanaka do.

"How long?" I ask.

"Fifteen minutes, maybe, before my influence wears off."

Fifteen minutes. That's... "You didn't use that on me, did you?"

"Doesn't work on us," Taggart says.

Good to know, but it makes me wonder. Do my new abilities work on him? I don't have a clear memory, or idea, of who's eyes I saw out of during the visions while on that table.

We reach the main floor, but Max leads us down one more flight to the parking garage.

Max swings the door open. The garage is full of black, Division Six vehicles. One, a Suburban, is running, the doors open wide. Someone sits in the driver's seat, but he isn't facing us, and I can't see who it is, not that I would know.

"In the truck," Max says.

I make my way past Max and head toward the nearest open door, which will seat me right behind the driver.

Max and Taggart rush to the other side of the vehicle and climb in.

As I shut my door, the driver turns and peers around the seat.

It's a woman. Her dark, brown hair is cut short, and her eyes are dark pools in the low light of the garage. She has a long scar running from near the corner of her right eye, against the line of her cheek, around the back of her neck where it disappears beneath her coat.

I've seen her before. I know it. But with all the extra memories in my head, the visions, I'm finding it hard to sort out my old memories from the noise.

"Nice to see you again, Steve," she says. "It's been a while."

"Come on, Sam," Max says, "get us out of here. You two can catch up later."

Sam.

The scar.

I can feel it down deep that I know who she is, but I just can't place her.

Twenty years of little change in my life, doing the same things day after day with the occasional interruption, until a week or two ago. God, I can't even tell how long it's been since I woke up to that sweet smell in the sewer and ran into Taggart. I've lost too many days. But in that time, I've lost a friend, gained new abilities, and I'm on the run from a global corporation that has dire sounding plans for me and everyone like me.

And here I am, upset because I can't remember how I know Sam.

She turns toward the front, depriving me of the opportunity to study her further, and puts the van in motion.

She zooms out of the parking garage and onto the nighttime streets. For the moment, we're free.

CHAPTER 27

By the time Sam delivers us to our hideout—a low, darkly painted rambler surrounded by an eight foot security fence—my ability to stay upright despite my swimming head has exhausted itself. The rest I managed to get in the Suburban while we drove only served to deepen my exhaustion. I practically fall out of the door when it opens, only staying on my feet by the luck of successfully grabbing at the door handle on my way down.

"You all right?" Sam asks.

"Yeah," I say. "I just need a moment." I'm not in any hurry to appear weak to a woman I feel I should know, but have no memory of.

"Right," she says.

She inserts herself under my arm. She's not weak. If she were any taller, I wouldn't doubt that she could lift me off the ground.

"Come with me," she says.

She pulls me toward the front door of the house. While she's carrying me, I notice that Max has climbed into the driver's seat of the Suburban.

"What's he doing?"

"He's going to ditch that beast. DivSix will track it down eventually, and when they do, we don't want it anywhere around here."

"He'll be back?" I ask.

"Eventually."

I haven't a clue what that means.

We ascend a pair of concrete steps, and then she palms a key card out of a pocket and slaps it across a reader on the front of the house.

"Brighten up," she says. "Put on a smile. We've just rescued you from certain slavery, and you've got guests."

"Guests?" I ask as the door swings open.

Sam guides me in through the door.

"Steve!" I hear shouted from across the room.

I look over to see Mary jumping up from a couch where she had apparently been sitting, reading a book.

She runs across the room, her face changing from surprise to concern in the process, and takes my other arm, lightening the burden on my legs, somewhat.

"Is he okay?" she asks.

"He's fine," Sam answers. "He needs rest."

"He looks like hell. Why is he still in a hospital gown?"

Damn, did I miss Mary. She'll have me dressed and comfortable soon.

"We didn't have time to put him in a suit," Sam says. I hear sarcasm in the voice, but there's a bit that sounds like she's defending herself. Who was she to me?

"What's Mary doing here?" I ask, hoping to stop any arguments that might spring up between them.

"We picked her and George up before we came to get you," Sam says. "DivSix would expect you to go to them first."

"They wouldn't have been wrong," I say.

"And it would have been a stupid thing for you to do," says George from somewhere behind me.

I can't summon the energy to respond.

They carry me down a hallway and then into a bedroom where they don't quite dump me on the bed. I don't even have the energy to check to see if my hospital gown has left me exposed in some embarrassing fashion. At this point, I hardly care.

Mary's hands gently adjust me so that I am more properly laying on the bed, and then she, I assume it's she since my eyes have closed, covers me with a blanket.

"Sleep well," she whispers in my ear. Then she kisses me gently on the forehead.

CHAPTER 28

At some point, I wake up.

A ray of sunlight sneaks past the thick curtains, splashing against the room's hardwood floor, exposing the wood's slightly reddish hue. After first noticing it, I quickly shift my gaze to the opposite wall, a habit built from years of pain avoidance.

But it slowly occurs to me that I hadn't felt any pain when looking at it, and I force myself to look at it again.

No pain. Not even a little discomfort. It's as if I am human again.

I look around the room. It's empty. I'm a little surprised that Mary isn't here waiting on me to wake, but then, maybe she was, and is now sleeping. I don't hear any other sounds of life in the house, no TV, no music, nothing. Doesn't mean someone isn't awake, though.

That's fine by me. I'll use the time to remember things, to sort out what I stole from Joe.

First, an experiment.

The light on the floor is calling to me like a fire on a cold night. I have to see.

I climb out of the bed, taking a blanket with me. They haven't replaced my hospital gown yet.

I feel stronger than I did the previous night. I wonder how long my recovery would have been if I hadn't taken Joe's life for my own. Slower, probably.

The spot of light on the floor lies a few feet away, and I approach it, half in excitement, half trepidation. But I have to know.

I kneel down when I get close, and then slowly reach out my hand until my fingertips enter the beam. I flinch a little as they enter, but the pain doesn't come.

I push my hand a little further in, until the light hits my palm. The light is warm, tingles a bit, but there is no pain.

Joe did what he said he would, what he'd hoped to do all these years, what I'd hoped for, but never really expected to have happen.

I'm cured.

I drop the blanket, which takes the hospital gown with it and leaves me naked, and walk to the windows. I pull the curtains open and bask in the sunlight. It's a long lost feeling that had faded so far into memory that I could only remember it through the memories of others. My own memories of the warmth of the sun were buried beneath thirty years of pain, but no longer.

"Yaahhh!" I shout.

The door opens behind me.

I spin around.

Sam is looking at me from the doorway, but shielding herself from the light with the door.

"What do you think you are doing? Shut the drapes!"

"I just…"

"Shut 'em!"

I turn and reach for the curtains, pull them toward me, and shut out the warmth of the sun.

I turn back around, and she throws some clothes at me. They hit me in the chest and fall to my feet.

"Put those on," she says.

I bend down and find khaki pants, black underwear, and a dark blue button-down shirt. I grab the underwear first, embarrassed only a little at standing naked in front of her. I notice she's not turning away.

"So he did it," she says as I dress. "He really cured you."

"Yes," I say. "It seems he did."

"Did you lose anything, like Max?"

"I don't think so," I say as I slip an arm into the shirt. "In fact, it seems I gained something."

I slip the other arm through and start buttoning it up. It seems to fit pretty well. Mary would have had my size.

"Gained something?"

"Yeah."

"Are you going to tell me, or are you going to make me dig for it?"

I look up at her. I can still see her face in the dim light just as well as ever. Joe's potion didn't take that away from me. She's beautiful, about my age. Of course, she's one of us, so she would be. The scar, instead of marring her beauty, only serves to give her a toughness that she would lack without it.

But I still can't remember who she is, where I should know her from.

"You still don't remember, do you?" she asks.

I try, really try, to find a memory of her, but if I have even one, it's been buried among the thousands of memories I've stolen from others.

"Twenty-eight years ago," she says, realizing I'm not going to answer, "you found me while I was going through my change."

Twenty-eight years ago, I was in the middle of the darkest period of my life.

"I don't remember much from back then," I say. "I've tried to forget it all."

Her lips flatline. "Apparently, you succeeded."

She steps into the room, shuts the door, and studiously avoids a pool of light that has made it past the hastily shut curtains as she heads for the bed.

She sits down on it, places her hands in her lap. Her dark eyes, I can see now, are big and black and deep as a well.

"When you found me, they were... they..." She takes a deep breath. "When you found me, you drove them off, but not before they gave me this scar."

I pick up the pants, now, and slip them on, acutely uncomfortable with how she found me now that I understood what had happened. It bothers me that I can't remember. I know I should. Anyone would remember that.

"That scar should have healed itself," I say to hide my discomfort with talking about what happened.

"I was just starting to turn. You took me to where you were hiding, gave me food, kept me warm, told me what was happening to me. You don't remember any of that?"

"No," I say.

She looks disappointed, not looking straight at me, as if she's slightly embarrassed, now.

I don't like standing here. There's a wooden, four legged stool in the corner of the room, so I drag it over in front of her and sit on it.

"Look," I say, feeling my way, "that was a long time ago. I hurt a lot of people back then . . . since then. I took a lot of memories."

"Your ability," she says.

"Yes."

"And the memories..."

"They drown things, bury them, and I tried to forget a lot of it."

"Did you try to forget me?" She almost looks vulnerable as she asks the question.`

"I can't imagine wanting to forget you, but for ten years, I wandered through my life with nothing but the pain of knowing I had lost my entire life."

She looks up at me sharply.

"You asshole," she says.

"What?"

"You save me, protect me, become my lover for a short while, then disappear on me, and you have the nerve to call it nothing?"

Lover? Shit.

"I... I..."

She stands up, looks down on me with righteous fury. Her scar pulses with her anger, and I feel like I'm in real danger.

"You had better stammer, Steve. It was only six months, but you kept me safe, you kept me sane while my body adjusted to the change, while I figured out my ability. You kept me alive.

"And you held me every night, made love to me in all the strangest of places, let me know I meant something to you."

I know I should know all this, but it's all gone. Only the vague recognition that I've seen her before remains.

"And then," she continues, "you left, and I didn't see you again."

I sit there. I can't do anything else. I sit and watch her through long moments of silence. I can hear her breath. I find myself hoping for my strange new ability to manifest itself so that I can see into her head, understand what she's thinking. But it doesn't happen.

"What? You don't have anything to say?"

"I can barely remember my childhood," I say. "I couldn't remember what walking in the sunlight like a normal person felt like until just a few moments ago, and that's the only memory I have of it. All the others are lost.

"It's not because of you. It's because of my ability. I wish I could recall that time, but it's gone. And now, I've got even more memories to deal with."

I realize, immediately, that I shouldn't have said that, but she doesn't say anything. Perhaps she doesn't realize the significance. Taggart and Max probably still think Joe was killed in the firefight. I'd like to have it remain that way.

She inhales deeply, closes her eyes, then holds her breath for long moments before releasing it and lowering her chin to her chest as she does.

Eventually, she looks up again, and it's clear to me that she's made a decision in those moments.

"You don't even remember my ability, do you?"

"No," I say.

"Good," she says and smiles. "Then there's nothing in the way of us starting over."

"What?" What about Mary? What?

"We're two of a kind, Steve, and you're the only one of our kind that I can really stand. I work with Taggart and Max because of Joe, but I'd prefer to dump them out on the sidewalk and let them fend for themselves."

At the mention of Joe's name, my whole focus shifts from relationship issues back to the situation that I'm in.

"So," she says, stepping in close to me with an obvious sway in her walk, "why don't we get to know each other again."

I put my hand out to stop her and she rests up against it, my hand uncomfortably just below her breasts.

"Wait," I say. "Joe set you up with Taggart and Max?"

"Yeah," she says.

"How long have you known Joe?"

"Why?" she asks, letting up on the pressure against my hand.

I pull my hand away, though I'd like to leave it touching her. Of course, if Mary walked in on us, what would she think?

"Please," I say. "How long?"

"About twenty-five years, give or take."

This time, it's me that must take a deep breath.

"What's wrong?" she asks.

"That's about five years longer than I've known him."

"Yeah," she said. "I know."

"What do you mean you know?"

"I mean that I helped him find you, back then. I was desperate to find you. I loved you."

"How..." So many questions. I'm not even sure which ones to ask.

"How what?"

"How did you meet him?"

"I'd rather not say," she says.

She doesn't know yet that, given enough time, I could probably find out how. I just need to assimilate Joe's memories. Thinking about it brings the pressure of them to the fore. I have to do it soon.

"Please," I say. "I thought for twenty years that I was the only one of us he knew, and then two weeks ago, I find out he's working for a company that has an interest in us, and then I find out that company is partially responsible for us being the way we are. And now, Joe's dead and I'm cured, and I've got new abilities that I don't even know how to use and unless I can get some handle on what the hell is going on, I feel like I'll be torn apart. Please, Sam. Help me. Tell me about how you met Joe."

"Fine," she says. "I was on Aurora, selling my ass, when this old Chevy van pulls up, looks like it's right out of the seventies with the bubble shaped rear windows and the tie-dyed paint job and all.

"This guy leans out, he's losing his hair, I can tell, and he says, 'Excuse me, but are you Samantha Ringwold?' "

CHAPTER 29

"Excuse me. Are you Samantha Ringwold?"

I'm looking out through the passenger side window at an emaciated young woman with a scar running down the right side of her cheek and neck. She's wearing typical hooker garb, fishnet stockings, short, bright skirt, and a top that exposes what cleavage she's got on her thin frame. It's clear she hasn't eaten well in a while, and is probably strung out.

"What of it?" she asks. "You a cop? An investigator?"

I smile. "No," I say. "Nothing like that. I'm a friend of the family." Sort of.

"What happened?" she asks, scared now. "What happened to my mom?"

"Oh, she's fine," I say. I need to get her into the van, get her off whatever junk she's on, though it probably isn't hurting her near as much as it would otherwise. "She's just worried about you." Yes, it's a standard lie.

"Bullshit," she says. "I don't know you. Why do you assholes always have to be so creepy?"

She turns as if to walk away.

"Look, look," I say before she can slip away. "A hundred dollars. Anywhere you want. I just want to talk to you."

She turns back. A hundred dollars will probably feed her for a week, or her addiction for a day.

"A hundred? To talk?"

"Yes."

"You're crazy," she says, but I can see she's thinking about it.

"No. Not crazy, I just want to tell you some things I know about your past, maybe help you out, get you off the street."

"The street suits me fine." It's an argument she's probably used a thousand times to herself.

I push open the passenger side door.

"Does it?" I ask.

She looks at the door, then up at me, then down the street, looking for an out. I'm offering her more, but she's too damaged, I think, to understand that.

"Anywhere?" she asks.

"Anywhere but the side of the road," I say.

She grabs hold of the door for the first time, then pulls herself up and into the seat so fast that I have to sit back quickly. She pulls the door shut, then stares straight ahead.

"All right, Danny's, and you're buying dinner on top of the hundred."

"I can do that," I say.

"Steve?"

CHAPTER 30

"Steve?"

I blink, startled back to the now, into my own head. The memory came on so fast and strong, I lost myself in it.

"Steve? Were you even listening to me?"

"I was listening," I say.

I didn't need to listen. I was there, through Joe's memory, and while I don't seem to have my own memories of her, I now feel terrible for what happened to her after I left her.

"What did I say?" she asks.

"That Joe took you to dinner at Danny's, told you who and what he was, what he was doing, helped out out of the life that you had fallen into after I disappeared."

"You weren't listening," she says. "You're just... Wait. I never mentioned Danny's. I haven't even gotten to the part about the dinner. How did you know that?"

Shit. Caught.

Her eyes widen, her mouth drops open just a little as she realizes what's happened, as she puts the pieces together.

"Joe couldn't have told you," she says. "He wouldn't have. You claim you can't remember me, yet you know that stuff about me?"

I sit in silence. She'll come around to it, and I haven't even had time to deal with it myself. The enormity of what happened back in that room is still overwhelming.

She sits back down on the bed.

"No gunshot killed Joe," she says.

I still say nothing. Joe was my friend, long before I thought he betrayed me. Before last night, I hadn't killed a friend in twenty years or more.

"You did it."

Her accusation sits there uncomfortably between us. She knows she's right. I can feel it.

I look down at my hands, the hands that would be bloody had I used any normal method, the hands that took so many so long ago, and so few over the last twenty years.

An unexpected tear forms at the corner of her eye.

"Just tell me why," she says. Her voice is steady, though.

My fingernails need trimming.

"It was instinctive. When the lights went out, he brushed my hand with his arm and I grabbed at it. I was still feeling the effects of the treatment, and it just happened."

"You shouldn't have," she says.

"I know. I couldn't stop—can't stop once it's started. It's too late, then."

"You should have stopped. He was the only chance we had," she says.

And then I get it, or I get part of it. It's not just about a friendship with Joe for her, it's about something more, about getting her life back.

"He knew," I say. "He could have protected himself. He didn't."

She stands up, fury warring with frustration on her face.

"Dammit, Steve! You don't get it, do you? There are dozens of us still alive, and a dozen more or so in their *program!* Joe was trying to save us all! And now..."

She stands over me, breathing heavy, and I wait for the words that are running through her mind, but she never utters them, instead choosing to stomp her way out of the room.

The door slams behind her.

Could I have stopped?

I know the answer, but she's made me ask the question of myself, anyway.

I could have never started. I could have held off my need like I've done for so many years. But could I have? I try to think back, but the whole thing is a bit of a blur, a dark shadowy blur. The drugs, the visions, the blackout, the gunfire. I wasn't in control, and Joe had done that to me. Right? If Joe's death is anyone's fault, it's his, right?

But I'm not so sure, and I sit on the stool, staring at the rumpled bed with its light blue sheets and knit blankets, and replay the situation in my head. I could have not started.

The door opens behind me and I hear lighter footsteps than the ones Sam used to exit the room.

"Steve?"

I spin around on the stool at the sound of Mary's voice. She's looking at me with sympathy in her eyes. She knows what happened. She either heard us, or Sam told everyone.

Everyone. I'm not even sure who is all here except Sam, Mary, and George. I don't know if Max ever came back.

"Did you hear?" I ask, hoping that Sam kept it to herself.

"Sam told me," she says.

"Did she tell everyone?" I ask.

"Not yet. No one is awake but us three."

"Great," I say. Sam may still tell them all.

"She asked me to come talk to you."

"About what?"

"Just to talk with you," she says.

"Just to talk?"

"Yes," she says.

"Well, come sit down on the bed and we'll talk," I say.

"All right," she says.

Something doesn't seem right. She seems wary of me. Her answers are too short, to non-committal.

She steps around me, keeping her distance while trying hard not to look like she's keeping her distance. I can tell, though, because she keeps an eye on me as she moves.

When she finally sits, spreading the comforter out to her sides with her hands, we stare at each other for a couple minutes in silence, until I can stand it no longer.

"What did you want to talk about?"

"Did you really kill Joe?" she asks.

"Not on purpose," I say. "It was a reaction to a stressful situation."

"Does that always happen when you're under stress?"

"No."

Most of the time, I try to keep myself from being under any stress. This past couple of weeks, though, culminating in the experience in the lab with Joe, I haven't been terribly good at managing my stress.

"How did you kill him?" she asks, and I realize I have

never before told her all the details of my curse. I had hoped to keep them to myself.

"His hand brushed mine, and I grabbed it, and then I took…"

It hurts to think about it. The farther I get from the event, the more I find out about what Joe was doing, why he was doing it, the more I wish I had been able to stop myself, and the less I want to think about it.

"Took what?" she asks.

"Everything," I say. It's time Mary knew all about what I can do. Thinking about it, I should have told her about it last week when I was trying to keep her from going with me. Perhaps that would have scared her off.

"What's everything?"

"Everything that made Joe who he was. His life force, his memories, his energy. You could almost say that I'm carrying him inside me, now."

"Inside you?"

I nod.

"How many others?" she asks.

"Too many to count," I say.

Physically, she doesn't react at all, which surprises me. I expected her to be appalled.

"Do you carry them all with you?"

"Yes, though after a time, they start to blend together."

"When was the last time?" she asks.

"Before Joe?"

She nods.

I try to think back, to find my own memories among the ones that swirl around in my brain. Normally, it's easier to pull them out, but I still haven't assimilated Joe's memories, and it takes me longer than I would like to find the last time, the teenager that accosted me at a bus stop, that wouldn't leave me to myself, that pulled a knife on me when I wouldn't hand him my wallet.

"About three and a half years ago," I say.

"Was it an accident, then?" she asks.

"No," I say. Not that time. There were other accidents, though, long ago.

"You murdered someone on purpose?" The distaste with which she says that is something I can feel on my own tongue. I almost wish it *had* been an accident.

I shake my head. "It was self-defense," I say. "He tried to rob me at a bus stop."

"So you killed him."

"He pulled a knife on me."

She has nothing to say to that, and we stare at each other again.

What I wouldn't give for things to go back to the way they were, back when Mary was my girlfriend, back before the change. Hell, at this moment, I'd even take having them go back to the way it was just a few weeks ago when I knew what the score was, when I'd accepted what I'd become, when Joe was alive and none of us were in danger.

"Sam says all their plans are ruined since Joe died," she says.

The change of topic throws me.

"What?" is the best I can do.

"Sam says that, with Joe dead, there's no hope for the rest of them. I think she's angry that you got treated, but with Joe gone, there's no chance for treating the rest of them."

"That's not quite all she's angry about with me."

"She likes you, you know."

"We knew each other long ago," I say.

"As did you and I," Mary says.

I am now completely baffled at where she's going with this.

"Do you like her?"

Jealousy? Or competition?

"I don't know her," I say.

"You knew her before," she says.

"I don't remember. I buried those memories so long ago, that whole period of my life, I try to forget."

"You remember me."

"You were the last good thing I could remember happening to me."

"Tell me something," Mary says.

"What?"

"You tried to keep me from going with you. You tried to push me away, but you didn't seem like you really wanted to. Do you want me?"

"I did, I do, but what do I have to offer you? You've had a life, a family. What will they think when you start seeing a man that looks like he's thirty years younger than you?"

"What do you want now?" she asks.

Where the hell did this conversation go so totally off the rails?

"I can't follow what you want at all," I say. "First, you come in talking about Sam, and Joe, and wondering if I had really killed him, and then you find out how many I've killed, and I think you will be horrified, and it seems like you're leaning that way, and all of a sudden your asking if I still want to be with you? I don't get it, Mary."

"Do you think I get it?" she asks. "Yes, the things you've done scare me, but horrify? No. I understand what you are. Even though I didn't know you could do that, I've known there was some dark secret you were keeping from me, and I was willing to overlook that. I was in love with you, madly, and I couldn't wait to marry you. Then you disappeared. And right when my husband dies, you reappear to save me from my grief. I knew you were different. You told me some of what had happened. I could live with it, but you were so distant, so damaged, but I could tell you still cared.

"Then, you stumble into my apartment, drugged to the gills, and I thought you were going to die on my living room floor just like my husband. I knew then that, no matter what, I didn't want to lose you again. I don't want you to disappear on me.

"Yes, you look thirty years younger, but that's only looks. I can live with ridicule. I can live with people thinking you're my son instead of my lover, but what I can't live without is you. Never again. Whatever the cost.

"I know you don't want to kill people. I know you don't want to hurt them. From what you've told me, what I've overheard from Sam and the others, what happened to you all is not your fault."

She stands up and steps close to me. Her hands tremble.

"Standing this close to you scares me right now, now that I know what you can do, that I know you can kill me with just a touch. But you never did before."

"I won't kill you, Mary," I say. "Never."

"If you killed me that way, you would know what I know, remember what I remember?"

"Yes, but I won't do it, ever. You don't have to worry."

"Stand up," she says.

I follow her orders, and push the stool out of the way with my foot.

She puts her hands to my face and pulls my head down so that I am looking into her eyes.

"I know everything is a mess for you right now. I understand. But if you choose Sam over me, I want you to promise me one thing."

"I won't choose her," I say. "She doesn't..."

Mary covers my mouth with her hand until I stop talking.

"If you choose her, promise me that you'll never forget me."

"What?"

"Promise me that my memories will live on, that, when I'm eighty or whatever, or before I get Alzheimer's, you'll come and you'll kill me and take my memories so that I won't be unremembered, so that I'll always be with you."

I try to step back, but she's still holding me tight.

"Mary," I say.

"Promise me."

"I promise," I say, "but not now. When you're older. Much, much older."

"Of course, you nitwit."

Then she pulls my head down and kisses me, and her lips are soft and warm, her tongue just a bit more inquisitive than I remember, a bit more passionate, and she tastes like strawberries.

When we separate, it takes a couple of breaths before I can come back to myself.

"Now," she says. "I want you to lay down on that bed and try to remember everything Joe did related to the drugs he gave you. Sam and the rest deserve any help you can give them for saving you, and if what you're telling me is true, you should know how to make more of those drugs."

I should have thought of it myself. Sam should have thought of it. But I was, and still am, a bit muddled by the drugs and Sam was angry. Max? Max might have thought of it if he knew I had killed Joe. But it doesn't matter. I should have thought of it, and would have once I had assimilated all of his memories.

But I hadn't, and Mary had.

I pulled her close to me, and this time, I kissed her, and after we were done, she smiled.

"Thank you," I say.

"You're welcome," she says.

"I need food, and probably the rest of the day alone."

"Whatever you need," she says, and then walks past me to the door. Her fingers trail along my side until we're no longer touching.

I miss the touch immediately, but I have work to do, and, for the first time, I have some hope I can salvage the situation. I can make a difference.

Once the door closes behind her, I lay down on the bed and start sifting through my newly acquired memories, hoping I can find the key to curing us all.

CHAPTER 31

I emerge from the room hours and hours later, perhaps even a day later. I'm exhausted.

I walk down the short hallway toward the living room, and find Sam and Mary and Max sitting, all looking at me. They had to have heard the door open. I have no idea what they were doing before I emerged.

"Well?" Mary asks.

"I haven't found them, yet," I say.

I can see the disappointment on the faces of Mary and Sam. Max's face is impossible to read, but he doesn't have much invested in the outcome of what I can find, anyway. The damage has already been done to him.

"How long will it take?" Sam asks. She's assuming that I will find them.

"It can take a week or more," I say.

"They'll be in there, though, right? You'll find them?"

"There's no guarantee I'll find anything."

"You don't have a week," Max says.

"What do you mean?"

He shifts in his seat.

"They are out there looking for us, looking for you. And Taggart, if you don't find the answer in three or four days, Taggart will have to return to them, or he'll die."

Three or four days. That tightens the noose a bit.

"Where is Taggart?" I ask.

"Out with George, getting supplies," Sam says.

George. I had completely forgotten about him. I haven't even talked to him since I came here.

"Well, if anyone has got some food, and something to drink, I'll get back to searching."

Sam gets up off the couch and says, "Come with me."

I follow her into the kitchen. It's well appointed, with a granite counter-top, dark, hardwood cabinets, cleaned to the point that you wouldn't worry about eating off any surface. Not that I'd worry, but Mary could.

"It's nice in here," I say. "This whole house, is nice."

"Thank you," she says. "I've got leftover chicken, or I could cook you up a steak in about fifteen minutes."

"I'll take the chicken," I say, conscious of the need preserve what time I have.

She opens the door to the refrigerator, a stainless steel monstrosity, and starts searching through it. There's no light in the refrigerator.

After a moment, she pulls out a plastic bag that's got three pieces of fried chicken in it.

"Do you really think you can do it?" she asked.

"If it was important to him, it's in my head, now. It just takes time to sort through a lifetime of memories."

She pulls out a small plate from a cabinet and dumps the

chicken out on it, then turns to a microwave and punches in two minutes.

"You can't just go to the latest memories and search through those?"

I can already smell the chicken.

"No. Memories aren't ordered that way. We attach importance to them, tags, if you will, that help us search our own memories. When I take someones memories, I'm not always able to understand what that person's tags mean, how they're ordered, until I've seen enough of their memories to start making connections."

"How long does that usually take?"

"A day or two, if I'm lucky, if their memory is in good shape. If they're older, sometimes it takes much longer."

"Joe?" she asks.

"He was older, but I don't think his memories have deteriorated. He just has a lot of them he deems important."

"What have you found so far?"

"His most cherished memories seem to be the times he found one of us, me, you, others. Then I've seen a few of the discoveries he made, but they're all disjointed so far. I don't know enough to understand them all."

"That worries you," she says.

The microwave dings and shuts off. She opens the door, and the smell of the chicken makes my mouth water.

"It does," I say as she hands me the plate. It's hot, but not a bother.

"Why?"

"What if I find the set of memories that I'm looking for, what if I find them and don't understand them? What if I miss them because I don't understand what I'm looking at?"

"Does that happen?"

"Yes," I say. "Memories always have a context, and sometimes, that context is not important enough to make a lasting memory."

"Joe helped you figure this all out, didn't he?"

"Yes. I'm really sorry, Sam. I didn't mean to kill him."

"I know you didn't," she says. "You may not remember what happened back then, you may not remember me or us, but I do. And I remember how you struggled to control that part of you. Joe had told me that you had learned to control it, that it didn't rule you anymore."

"It doesn't, most of the time."

She turns away from me, back to the fridge. "You want a beer?"

A beer. I haven't had one in so long. I stopped drinking when I realized alcohol no longer affected me.

"No thanks," I say. "I need to be able to think. Water is fine."

She pulls a glass down from a cupboard, takes it to the fridge and fills it with water from the dispenser on the front.

She brings it back and hands it to me. Her fingers briefly touch mine as I take it from her.

"I missed you," she says.

"I..."

"Shh. Even when Joe told me he had found you, he told me I should have no contact with you, that you were dangerous, but that you were also the key to finding a cure, to freeing us from our private hells. He wouldn't tell me how to find you."

The key?

"Did he ever say why he thought I was the key?"

"No," she says.

One more thing to puzzle out.

"Would you tell me one thing?" I ask.

"What?"

"What is your ability?"

"I can make people see things that aren't there," she says.

"Can you make them not see things?"

"Yes. It's not so useful to do that, though, when we can't leave the dark."

"Can you make yourself invisible?"

"I thought you were only going to ask one thing. Don't you need to eat?"

Her reaction surprises me. I didn't expect her to get defensive.

"Okay, one last question, I promise, and then I'll go do my homework."

"Shoot," she says.

"How many times were you at Joe's when I came by?"

Her eyes widen, then she looks away and turns her back to me.

"Sam?"

"Go eat," she says, "and then figure out how to make more of that serum before Taggart dies."

CHAPTER 32

I eat the chicken in my room. It surprised me that she wouldn't answer that question, but I can't make her. It's obvious, though, that she was standing in Joe's home lab at least once, if not more times, or she just would have told me it never happened.

After I finish the chicken, I set the plate on the floor beside the bed, swallow the last of my water, and lay down on the bed.

But thinking about Sam's lack of response puzzles me. Why wouldn't she answer? How many times did she deceive Joe and hide from him and me? Why? And why is she embarrassed about it?

I force myself to put those thoughts aside and start searching through Joe's memories again. Now that I know how urgent it is, despite what I told them, I think I can find them in time if I focus on getting them assimilated. What I told them is true, but I can't guarantee the memories are there, or that, if they were there, they're still there. The visions I had while on those drugs, who knows what they could have done to the memories.

So, I lay back, close my eyes, and try to remember.

What do I want to remember? I want to remember the formula. I want to remember how I made the serum.

I see notes on a pad of paper, lots of notes, scribbled in Joe's tiny hand. A desk lamp burns in the darkness of a late night. The notes are a mess of numbers and symbols that I have no context for. I tag the memory, though. I can look them up if I have to, but it isn't going to help us right away.

Another memory, then. Something in the lab.

The lab is brightly lit. There are half a dozen workers in bright yellow hazard suits, and I'm looking at them through thick glass walls.

"It shouldn't have happened," says Anna's voice.

"These things happen, sometimes," I say.

"You said this batch would be the one."

"I've been wrong before. Maybe the techs screwed something up. Maybe the temperature was too high. I won't know until the cleanup is completed."

"We don't have much time left, you know. He's not going to live forever."

"I have more reason to get this right than just Brad Archon," I say. "I'm doing my best."

Time to move on. That memory isn't going to help me, but I tag it, too. That Brad Archon is still alive, or was at the time of the memory, is news to me, and probably to the rest of the world.

I'm staring at a notebook, only this time, not at his desk. It's got some handwritten text in it, and after looking at it, I don't even have to read it. I remember what it says.

Steve,

I'm sorry I had to do this to you, but there is no other way. If you are remembering this, I am dead. Do not blame yourself. I intended for this to happen.

I know the others are probably angry with you, if they know, or are upset that I am dead and will not be able to follow up with cures for them, too, but I had little choice. I do not have access to a lab other than the one at Archon Global that is capable of making the cure, and I do not have any ability to leave the building with enough to cure all of my friends. They do not let me near the supplies, even though I am technically in charge of the project.

You are the key.

I burned all my notes, deleted everything on my hard drives and in the backups. But you can take my memories, find a lab and a few reputable scientists, and have them work out the solution.

Or, you can choose to bury it forever. It is your choice. Either everyone should have these abilities, or no one should. I know what Archon Global would do with it long term, and I know in the short term, they intended to bind you and the rest of the test group and sell your services to the CIA.

One last thing. Taggart will probably need the cure sooner than you can reproduce it. Archon Global has fifteen more doses in storage at the lab in anticipation of its success. I do not have the key code. Anna does not trust me with it anymore, but I know you and the new friends you must have should be able to help you get access.

Tell them I am sorry I could not tell them what I planned, but I could not risk being locked in at Archon Global while they enslaved you in an effort to corner the market on global espionage.

Goodbye,

Joe

Then I rip the sheet from the notebook, stand up and cross the room to my fireplace, then throw the paper in the fire and watch it burn.

CHAPTER 33

"You want me to believe he died on purpose? That he committed suicide by you?" Sam asks.

We're standing in her living room again, only this time, Max is absent, but Taggart and George have returned. Taggart sits on a giant leather footstool that's shaped like a cube. George stands in the corner by the door, and Mary sits on the couch, fingernails in her mouth.

"Yes," I say. "He wrote it all down on a sheet of paper, then read it over and over until he remembered it word for word, then tossed it in the fire. And the letter said he did it on purpose. He swears they would not have let him leave."

"I could have made them," Taggart says. "I made Anna."

"I can only tell you what it said."

"So you can make the serum?"

"I can't. Not in time to save Taggart, but there are fifteen other doses at the lab."

"Why didn't he tell us that?" Sam asks. "We could have brought it out with us."

"I don't know," I say. "I only know what was in the note."

"So how do we get this extra supply?"

"Anna has the keycode. She wouldn't give it to Joe."

"That woman doesn't trust anyone," Taggart says. "Ever since Mr. Archon died, she's been extra secretive."

"You were around when Brad Archon died?"

"Yeah," Taggart says. "He was crazy insane from the drug, and one day, he up and jumped from the building."

"Did you see it?"

"No. It was at night. No one I know saw it, but we all heard about it."

"He's not dead," I say, remembering the conversation with Anna in the lab.

"Bullshit. He's dead. Hasn't been seen or heard from in years," Sam says.

"One of Joe's memories is a conversation between Joe and Anna, and Anna clearly says they need to get the serum ready because Brad Archon doesn't have long to live, and the memory felt recent."

"When?" asks Taggart.

"It's hard to tell, but no more than a year ago. Could have been weeks ago."

"Your certain of this?" asks George.

"Yeah, why?"

"I was on duty the night he jumped. His face was crushed so badly by the fall, he could only be identified by the clothes he was wearing, his DNA, and the statement by Anna that he had gone missing an hour earlier."

"The DNA was a match?" asks Sam.

"Dead on match," George says.

"What does this really matter?" Taggart asks. "When do we go get my cure?"

"We need the key, first," I say.

Taggart jumps up from where he is sitting.

"I can make Anna give us the key. We can go right now."

"Can either of you go out in daylight?" I ask.

They both look at the window, but the curtains are shut. A faint glow outlines them, against the wall.

"I can," Taggart says.

"But Sam can't, and Max isn't back yet. We need Max, I think."

"I'll help, too," George says.

I can't let him do that.

"No, George. You stay here with Mary, keep her safe."

"I can still shoot better than you," he says.

"What's that matter. I can't shoot at all. There won't be any shooting. We'll be going in at night, and we can hide ourselves far better than you. Please, George. I don't want to lose another friend to this."

George tilts his head to the side and purses his lips as if to say, "Really?" I ignore it.

"So what's the plan?" Sam asks.

"I don't have a plan, but as soon as Max gets back, we'll make one."

"Then we should all get some sleep," Sam says. "Max will be back this afternoon, and we'll plan then."

Everyone assents, and begins to leave the room, or settle into the couches and chairs for a nap.

Sam turns to go to her room, but before she leaves, she looks at me in a way that I can't quite interpret. It seems she's asking if I'm going to come with her, but at the same time, it seems a warning, as if she still doesn't believe that Joe used me to kill himself.

I look from Sam, then down at Mary, and back. I'm not ready to go to bed. I've been lying down forever, it seems—first at the lab, and now in her back room while trying to recall a dead man's memories.

"I'm going to step out back for a moment," I say.

Sam turns away from me, and says as she heads down the hallway, "Don't stay out too long, and don't go out front." It's the first time I've felt like a teenager in years.

CHAPTER 34

Clouds cover the sky above me, but off to the west, I can see a hint of blue. Perhaps it will roam my way before I step back inside. Even without it, the energy from the sun that squeaks past the cloud layer feels good on my skin. It has been so long. The little taste I got in my room was wonderful, but this, this is unfiltered by glass.

"You're so white, you stay out very long, you'll get a sunburn."

I turn around. George has followed me out.

"You know," I say, "I wonder about that. What will happen to me now that I'm cured? Will I age like normal? Will my body stop repairing itself? Will I die from blood loss or disease?"

"What do Joe's memories tell you?"

"I haven't found any memories that answer those questions."

I turn back around and face Sam's backyard again. The deck George and I are standing on isn't very large, but a larger concrete area surrounds it. There are flower boxes around the edges filled with purple and gold flowers that I can't identify. Well kept grass covers the rest of the yard.

"I wonder how she does it," I say.

"Does what?"

"Keeps her yard groomed. I can't imagine she runs a lawn-mower at night."

"Friends," George says. "You could have had this, too."

"Please," I say. "I was fine."

"You were existing, barely. Look at what she's got, here."

"I have been looking. She's had a home, a life, all these years. She's not wealthy, by any stretch of the imagination, but she's done well, protected herself."

"You admire that," George says.

"I do. But..."

"But what?"

I look up at the sky again. The blue patch I saw is inching toward us.

"But she's had help. Joe told her who he was, what he was doing. She knew all along. They've all known all along, but he kept it a secret from me."

"Perhaps he had a reason," George says. "After all, with that note he left for your memories, he certainly seems to have had a plan, and it seems to have been fairly long term."

Perhaps.

There are a couple of white plastic lawn chairs off to my right. I take a seat in one of them. George takes a seat in the other one, his ex-cop weight bowing the legs just a little. I look out into the yard and watch the slight breeze blow across the lawn.

"The note he left for me was mostly about his instructions. He doesn't detail why," I say.

"Don't pull the pity party thing on me. You know, now, that Joe had a plan for you. He hid you, kept you a secret…"

"No, he didn't hide me, or keep me a secret. He told Sam about me, told her to stay away. The others knew, too, I think. He kept everything a secret from me. He kept me in the dark."

"Sorry, my friend, but you kept yourself in the dark. We all tried to help you, to get you to come in and stay in. How many times did I offer you a permanent room?"

I don't want to answer. The offer had come at least once a year, if not more, since we met.

"Right. You know it. You only have yourself to blame, and Sam, here, is proof. You could have done what she has done. You could have stayed with me, found a job, had a life."

I turn my head just enough so that I can look into his eyes as I speak. "I could have done all those things, but for how long? A day, a week? How long before I lost control of my need and took someone, killed them? Sam can do this, can live a life, because she doesn't have that ability."

"You've learned control," George says.

"Have I? I took Joe!"

"He did that, not you. He deliberately put himself and you in a position where he *knew* what would happen. I know you are blaming yourself, but don't. Nobody else does."

"Sam does," I say, and look up at the sky. The blue patch has shrunk and veered north of us. I won't be seeing the sun today.

"What is this with you and Sam?" George asks, deliberately using my comment about Sam to change the topic. "I thought you and Mary..."

The sky wavers, George's voice fades to nothing, and then I cannot see the backyard any more, but I'm looking at the front gate through a car window. The front gate is shut, and I can see only a tiny sliver of the house through it.

"Are you sure he's in there?" a voice asks. It sounds like it's coming through an earpiece, and I don't recognize it.

"Yes. The Suburban went in, left, and then drove to another location, but there was no sign of anyone other than the driver at that other location."

"And you had forensics check the Suburban?"

"Yes. He was inside at some point, and she was with him."

"All right, keep an eye on the place. Angstrom and the team is still with the Archon people. I can't extract him without alerting them. We need this one..."

"Steve!"

My vision shifts back, the backyard comes back into focus. What the hell?

"Are you okay?" George asks.

"I'm fine," I say, though I'm not sure if I am. That transition makes me a little dizzy.

"What the hell happened? I was talking, and it was like you went unconscious on me."

I take a moment to reign in the dizziness before I answer. It also gives me time to think about what I saw, and what I saw doesn't bode well at all.

I look up, then around the backyard, past the fence and hedges. I don't see any surveillance, but I'm not even sure what I would be looking for, and the guy was out front.

I get out of my chair and head for the door.

"We have to get inside," I say.

"Why?"

"They're watching us."

CHAPTER 35

Sam dresses herself on the other side of her bedroom door while I wait.

"How do you know it's not just some dream you had?" Sam asks.

"I don't, not really," I have to admit. "But George says I just blacked out for over a minute, which is just about as long as my vision, or whatever it was, lasted."

The door opens, and Sam steps out, dressed in black—black pants, black blouse, black tennis shoes. She has her hair pulled back again, which exposes her scar, and she's got a gun on her hip.

"You never had that ability before," she says.

"It's...new," I say.

"New? We don't get new abilities."

She walks past me and down the hall.

"I had visions while Joe was giving me the drugs, but after that night, I haven't had any more. I had thought they were a side-effect of the treatment."

She stops at a door that I haven't seen opened.

"But now you've had another."

"We could send Taggart, or maybe George out to check." George makes more sense. The CIA, or whoever it was, but I was betting on CIA, might now Taggart, but probably don't know George.

"No need," she says.

She opens the door.

Inside what was once a relatively large coat closet, she has built a command center for one. A rack of monitors show views of her property and the streets around her home. A computer sits below them, as well as a joystick and a large bank of hard drives in a rack.

She takes a seat in front of the computer.

"You say he was out front."

"Yes."

"Hmm, that would be what, sometime in the last fifteen minutes?"

I feel George crowd in behind me.

"Impressive," he says.

"Yes, fifteen minutes at most," I say.

She runs through a series of steps, and then a shot of the street in front of the house comes up on her monitor. It's empty.

Silently, I'm hoping it remains empty. I'd rather have the vision be a dream than reality. When all we were dealing with was Archon Global, it had the feeling of being too big to handle. But if the CIA knows who I am, if they're looking for me now, then I have bigger problems.

We wait, watching the street. Several cars drive by, but

not one of them stop long enough to have been the car in my vision.

After five minutes, I begin to feel that maybe we're lucky. Maybe it was just a dream.

And then a red Ford Taurus pulls over on the other side of the street. The windows are tinted, so it's hard to get a good look at the man behind them through the monitor.

Sam zooms in on the window, and we can see movement behind the window that looks suspiciously like he's watching the house through binoculars.

"That him?" she asks.

"I don't know. I didn't see him. I saw through someone's eyes."

Sam's head jerks towards me, and she seems to scrutinize me. "You can see what people are seeing? From inside their heads?"

The car starts to move.

"Look," I say, and she turns back to the monitor.

As the car drives away, she switches to another camera shot, and we can clearly see the license plate.

"A government plate," George says.

"CIA," Sam says.

"Most likely," George says.

Sam turns away from the computer to face me again.

"Now tell me, can you really see from inside someone's head?"

"Yes," I say. "I can hear, too, and sometimes, it seems like I get what they're thinking."

"Can you do this when you want?"

"I don't know," I say. "I haven't tried."

"Try it now," she says.

"Don't we have to leave?" I ask.

"Not yet," she says.

"Why not? They're coming for me, and for you."

"Trust me," she says. "We have time."

"Fine," I say, "but I don't even know where to start. The visions just happen."

"Think about it, Steve. If you can get into someone's head, hear what they're saying, what they're thinking, we could know exactly what's happening, why they're following us, if they're following us."

It makes sense. If I could just pick a person and see from inside their head, it would give us a huge advantage.

"Okay, but out on the couch. I need to sit down for it."

The three of us head out to the living room.

"So, who do I try it on?" I ask.

"Try George," Sam says. "He'll probably be easier."

Easier, or she doesn't want me looking inside her head. It doesn't matter.

I lean back into the couch and close my eyes. The vision outside had come while I was looking at something, but the others, my eyes were closed. It probably doesn't matter, but I can only imagine it will be easier with them shut.

And at first, nothing happens.

But I'm not really trying. I'm sitting, trying to open myself to let the vision come to me, but I get nothing.

"Anything yet?" Sam asks.

"Quiet," I say.

I reach out with my senses, try to find the people in the room. I've done this before, but rarely have I tried to do it consciously. It's one of the things that helps me see in the dark. I can feel them near me, George and his heavy breathing, Sam and her conscious energy. I can smell her, too, though not like I used to.

The memory of her smell comes to me all of a sudden, and it unlocks those memories of her that I had buried. Unearthed, they swarm up to overwhelm me—saving her, the first time we kissed, the first time we made love, the times we just held each other in the dark under the freeway. Her stench, my stench, the stench of our kind, the pheromone that we put off to warn others of our kind away, it had no effect on us. We ignored it.

And then the waking up, my hand on her skin, catching myself at the last moment as my need for life nearly overcame my need to have her with me. I had saved her, and had just come near killing her.

I got up and ran. Never came back, and she didn't know.

"Is something wrong, Steve?" Sam asks, breaking into the memories.

I open my eyes. There's a tear on my cheek.

"No," I say. "I just—you don't smell the same to me, anymore."

"What?" she asks.

"Never mind," I say, and I shut my eyes again. "I'll tell you later."

I work to shut those memories off without locking them away completely. They're getting in the way right now, but I want to relive them, learn what happened between us, figure out why she smells different now.

But that's not what I'm trying to do this minute.

I take a deep breath, and empty my mind. I think momentarily that a mental picture of him might help, but I toss that away. It's not the outside of him that I see, when

I'm looking through their eyes. I'm actually in them, a part of them, it seems. Maybe I need to try to *be* him.

I reach out for him with my mind, feel for him. I try to imagine what it's like being him, his size, his weight, his past, what he's doing right now. Nothing.

I don't give up, though. Sam is right. If I can do this, if I can learn to do this, what triggers it, how to go in, get out, I would have a huge advantage over the people chasing us. Knowing what they know, what they're thinking.

But when I saw through people's eyes back in the lab, I wasn't looking for them. The visions just happened. Why? What do I need to make them happen when I want them to happen?

Need.

The word sticks out to me.

An answer?

Need?

What did I need when lying there on the table?

A way out.

A way to stop the pain.

And I saw those things through the eyes of some of the people in the room. Through Joe, through Max or Taggart. I'm not sure about the technician, or the view I had of Miss Tanaka.

I hear Sam shift in her seat, her breath. I can smell her. No. Focus on the task.

What do I need?

I need to know what you are thinking.

I need to know what you see.

I need...

My vision shifts.

I see myself sitting back on the couch, leaning back. My eyes are closed, my mouth slightly open. I need to shave. Strange. I haven't had to shave in thirty years.

"He did it," George says.

I look up. George is sitting on the other side of my body.

"You sure? He just looks like he fell asleep."

"That's exactly what he looked like outside."

I'm not in George. I'm in Sam.

He still looks like he's asleep.

"How long?"

"Who's to say?" George says. "It was a minute or less, outside."

"Did he wake up on his own?"

"No, I think I shouted at him."

"We'll give him another thirty seconds to wake up. Hear that, Steve? Thirty seconds."

Thirty seconds. If you don't wake up, I'll kiss you. That should wake you up.

The vision shifts, my eyes pop open. Dizziness comes over me at the shift. It seems that will be something to expect.

But Sam's last thought, that was unexpected.

I look first to Sam, wondering if she really would have kissed me. The look on her face seems to show a bit of disappointment that fades quickly.

"Well?" she asks.

"I did it."

"Tell me," she says.

"George said, 'He did it,' and then you said, 'You sure? He just looks like he fell asleep.' "

"You could have heard that," she says.

"I know, but I didn't. I saw my body laying on the couch between you two."

I don't know why I'm trying not to let on that I was in her head and not George's. Perhaps it's because she seemed to not want me in her head. I don't want to upset her.

"What was he thinking?"

"I don't now. I don't think he was thinking anything. If he was, I didn't catch it."

She looks disappointed again.

"He doesn't need to prove it to us," George says. "Your street cameras proved he can do it. All he needs to do is be able to do it when he wants, and to who he wants."

There's the problem. I didn't get in the head of who I wanted.

Or did I?

I was thinking about her right before it happened, not George.

"Can you do it to the CIA man?" Sam asks.

I close my eyes.

"I can try."

Sam's scent still distracts me. What is it about that. In the past, it would have driven me away, but now, now I can't stop thinking about her. I'm thinking less and less about Mary. Mary, who I had wanted for so long, but couldn't have. Mary, who I had left when my change came over me, who I had found again, who I didn't want to hurt. She wants to be with me, and I wanted to be with her, but now I can only think of Sam.

Stop.

Stop thinking about them.

What had done it.

Need.

I need to know what the CIA man is doing. I need to know what he's thinking.

Everything shifts, warps, and snaps into place.

I look out the windshield, over the top of a red hood, down the street. In the distance, off to the right, the front gate of Sam's home. I smell the coffee that's still in its cup and has gone cold, the cigarettes in the ashtray.

Come on, Dan, where are you.

Shit, he's waiting for someone.

"Dan, ETA?" I say.

"Three minutes," Dan says in my earpiece.

Shit. Wake up. It's time to go.

I can't go.

I lift the cold cup of coffee to my lips. As it goes down, I realize it's not quite cold, but it's getting close enough that I don't want another sip.

"Oh, here's the update on the one named Max," says Dan.

"Listening."

"He pulled some nifty double back trick down on Denny. Lost us among the traffic."

"You lost him?"

"Yeah."

Good, Max is safe, but he's not coming here.

I need out.

Everything warps, the dizziness returns, and my eyes flutter open.

I try to sit up, but the dizziness makes it difficult. I sway a little, then crash back onto the couch to try to steady my head.

But I don't have time for that.

"Help me up," I say.

"Why?" George asks as he slips an arm under me.

"We have to get out now. We have two minutes before they arrive."

CHAPTER 36

Sam doesn't question me.

"Wake up!" she shouts into the house, then jumps up and starts running down the hallway.

"Head for the back yard!" echoes back to us as she disappears.

I hear her banging on the doors as George helps me to my feet.

"Looks like we're going with you," George says.

I groan. My head swims, just like it did back at the Division Six complex.

"Is my head always going to act like this after I do that?" I ask.

George laughs. "It's probably a good trade," he says.

"You wouldn't think so if it were you."

"It is what it is. Come on."

He helps me maneuver around that cubic footstool—it somehow placed itself in our way—and into the dining room area which will lead us to the back door.

I hear people in the rest of the house, Taggart and Mary and Sam, making a commotion.

Taggart emerges from the room that I had been using.

"What's going on?" he asks.

"CIA, two minutes," George says, then ushers me past the dining room table and up to the sliding glass door.

"How long til you can walk on your own?" George asks.

"Another minute or three?" I don't know the answer.

"Hope it's not much longer than that. I can't run and carry you at the same time."

"You can still run?" I ask.

"Hey, not fair."

Someone will have to tell me, one day, why humor seems so appropriate at the worst times.

George gets the door open, and we stumble out onto the back deck.

Taggart comes up behind us.

"Need help old man?"

"If you would," George says.

Taggart takes me from George, and practically lifts me off the ground with his arms.

"What's wrong with you?" he asks as he starts to carry me across the yard toward the hedges at the rear.

"Dizzy," I say.

"From the cure?"

"I don't know." I don't think I want him to know just yet what I can do. It's always been a habit to keep my abilities a secret, and I'm not sure it's a habit I want to break.

"I'm glad there's cloud cover today. The closer I get to needing my dose, the more it hurts."

We reach the hedge, and he sets me down.

"Can you stand here?" he asks.

"Yeah," I say, and lean back against the hedge.

"Good. I'm going to help Sam."

And then I remember, the sun will hurt Sam. Thick clothes and sunglasses only help so much. She'll be okay as she walks, but she'll be in pain the whole time.

"How long has it been?" I ask George. My sense of time seems skewed by my inter-body travels.

"It can't be more than a minute."

Which means it probably has. The way my luck has run, the CIA is standing right behind this fence.

Mary comes out of the back door carrying a dark gray backpack. It's not large enough to hold more than a day or two of clothing.

She runs across the backyard and joins us.

"What's in there?"

"I don't know. Sam told me to bring it. What's going on?"

"CIA is out front. We think they're coming for us. What's keeping them?"

We have to be out of time now.

In fact, I can hear the sounds of half a dozen cars pulling to a stop in front of the house. The sounds of doors opening echo through the neighborhood.

Taggart appears at the back door of the house, and he's carrying what looks like a body bag with him.

Sam.

Taggart rumbles across the lawn as quick as he can while carrying body bag Sam in his arms. I want to go help him, but I'd be useless.

"Open the fence," he says when he's about half-way across the lawn.

The fence?

"What fence?"

"Reach through the hedge. There's a gate on the other side."

I reach through like he said, and find, just like he said, a fence. Chain link, buried in the hedge.

I lift the latch, by feel, and the gate swings away from me.

"It's open," I say.

"Go through. There's a garage on the other side."

I get it now.

As long as the CIA hasn't blocked the garage.

I push through. The dizziness has ebbed a bit, and I can walk on my own, though I have to take care. Moving my head too quickly still makes it swim.

I hate the scratchy feel of hedges, the spiderwebs you inevitably find with your forehead, or worse, your mouth. The one I find happens to cover my whole face, and I instinctively reach up to brush it away. I hope the spider wasn't in it, but I can't stop myself from swiping at something that feels like the tiny legs of a spider crawling across my forehead.

On the other side of the hedge, beyond the fence, I find a tiny walkway, walled off on either side by a seven foot tall wooden fence. The walkway leads to the door of what must be the garage Taggart mentioned.

I get to the door, look down, and notice the door has no keyhole. There's an entry card reader next to the door.

"The door's shut," I call out.

"Just open it," Taggart says. "It's unlocked."

Of course.

I grab the knob and turn it. It opens. Sam must have unlocked it from the house.

Inside the garage, it's dark. There aren't any windows. Not surprising considering who owns it.

It takes my eyes a moment to adjust before I can see the details of the van that is hidden in the garage. It's black, probably seats ten people, and has no windows in the back portion. The side door is wide open, as if waiting for just this emergency. Briefly, I wonder why she has a van when she lives by herself, but the others pile into the garage behind me, and I have to get out of the way.

Once Taggart enters, he shuts the door. I hear it click as it locks, followed by the sound of a servo in the wall by the door. A hidden deadbolt.

Dim lights come on.

"Well," Taggart says, "Get in the van. George, you drive."

"Right."

I climb in the side door and find that benches line the walls of the van, except where the door is. I take a seat toward the back. A wall stands between the driver and the passenger compartment. It has a door, but the door lacks a window.

She had this built for transporting people like us during the daytime. My only question is how you get that many of us in the same place at one time.

Mary climbs in after me and sits to my left. I hear the zip of a zipper, and Sam emerges from her body bag and climbs into the back of the van, taking a seat across from me.

"I really hate that thing," she says. "Makes it hard to breathe."

Taggart jumps in, throws the body bag up against the far wall, and shuts the door. Then he opens the door to the cab and somehow slips his huge frame through the thin opening. He shuts it behind him.

The van starts, the rumble of its motor muffled to a degree by the door between it and us.

"You had this prepared already," I say.

"I did."

"For this?" Mary asks.

"Or something like it."

The van lurches backward, over a bump, and then comes to a stop. The gear shifts, my weight is thrown backward a bit. We are moving.

"Something like it?" I ask.

"I wanted a way out, in case Division Six came for me. I can't travel during the day, but Max can, Taggart can, Joe could. They could drive me, or anyone like us, anywhere we wanted to go at a time Division Six would expect us to be hiding from the sun. The benches pull out to make a bed so we can sleep, if necessary."

Visions of Sam and I sleeping together pop into my head, but they're not visions this time. They're memories. The memories that had come out during my attempt to get into George's mind. My body wants to explore them, remember what it was like to feel her, but a bump in the road interrupts the memory and brings me back to the present.

"Where did you go, just then?" Mary asks.

"What?" I ask.

"Your eyes, they glazed over for a moment, as if you were somewhere else. You had a smile on your face."

She noticed.

"Just a memory," I say.

"Of what?"

I glance at Sam, see her watching me, but look away just as quickly. I'm not ready to let Mary know about the feelings I'm finding for Sam when I haven't figured them out for myself.

"Just something that happened a long time ago." And then I try to change the subject quickly. "Sam, where are we going?"

"We're going to meet up with Max," she says.

"They were following him," I say.

"He lost them."

"They could have found him again."

She laughs. "Relax. They won't find him again. Once he gives you the slip, you stay slipped."

I hope that's the case.

"Are we going to try to get the doses tonight?"

"Yes," she says.

"They'll be waiting for us."

"Haven't you noticed, Steve," Sam says, her tone flat and dangerous. "They're always waiting for us. But they won't be ready for us."

I hope she's right.

CHAPTER 37

George drives us to a motel just about a mile from the Airport. A dive, one of those two story jobs without interior hallways. In the movies, the cops always show up at these things, but I guess there's an advantage in that there's always an easy way out, too.

He parks the van and shuts the engine off.

"We're staying here?" I ask.

"No," says Sam. "Just picking Max up."

"He live here?"

"Not a chance."

Her tone and the short response cause me to look up at her, but she's not looking at me. She's looking up at the door that divides us from the cab. She seems lost in her head a little. I find myself wondering what she's thinking.

"How long do we have to wait?"

"Twenty minutes or so," she says, but she doesn't look my way.

And then it occurs to me, I don't have to wonder what she's thinking. I can find out.

"I'm going to take a nap," I say.

"Fine," she says.

Something is really bothering her.

I move all the way to the back of the van so I can lean up into the corners. Mary looks at me oddly, probably wondering why I just don't lean on her, but to do this, I think leaning on her would be too much of a distraction.

When I get myself comfortable, I close my eyes and begin to focus on need. I need to know what is happening in Sam's head. I need to know what's wrong, what she's worried about.

The shift happens quicker this time. I seem to be getting the hang of it.

Looking through her eyes, I see the same interior of the van that I had been looking at for the last hour.

What's taking you so long, Max?

Her worry eats at her, at me.

You said you would be here.

She looks around, looks at Mary, then back at me. I'm slumped in the corner, looking pretty much like I've gone to sleep.

How can he go to sleep so fast with everything going on?

This is hardly what I hoped to find her thinking. The Max bit was important, but...

Sam looks at Mary, who is also watching me.

Too bad Mary's here. It would be nice to crawl up next to him and take a nap.

I wish I could figure out where he stands with her. Her feelings are obvious, but his. What I wouldn't give to get inside his brain.

Then she looks back at me, really looks at me.

He's not...

Time to get out.

I don't let my eyes open, and I keep breathing slowly, trying not to change anything I'm doing. The dizziness sweeps over me, which makes staying still more difficult. I would have fallen over, I'm sure, were it not for the walls of the van holding me up.

I can almost feel her eyes on me, wondering if I was doing what I was doing. I wonder if it would piss her off if she knew. The way she's changed, become stronger since that younger version of herself that I had saved from those savages, I wouldn't put it past her to make sure I felt pain for intruding on her thoughts.

Yes, better to not let people know what I can do. Keep it secret.

"Steve?" she asks.

I continue to pretend to be sleeping.

"Steve," she says again, a little louder.

I work on maintaining my breathing at the same rate. My heartbeat is simple, it continues to plod along, as it has done ever since the change. That is one thing that's constant, even after the cure.

Cure.

Joe didn't cure me.

He changed me.

Again.

"He falls asleep quick," Mary says.

"I guess so," says Sam.

I'm in the clear, for now.

But, if I can't look inside her head, maybe I've got some time to explore my memories of her so that they don't pop out at an inopportune moment.

I start sifting through them, skipping past the one where I rescued her. I don't need to see her that way again.

Instead, I start looking for the good moments, the ones that kept us together, the ones that made me feel about her the way I seem to.

But there isn't just one memory that defines our relationship. As I replay them, there are tender moments where I hold her while her body struggles with the change, where the pain of it threatens to overcome her mind like it had once done to me. There are times where we hold each other against the cold of the night. And the first time she told me about her family, how they had driven her out, not because of the change, but because of her drug use. And how, at first, she had thought the change was just a side-effect of the drugs, so she stopped. But the change just kept happening.

A hundred moments like these brought us together, kept us together.

Until the night I almost killed her.

The sound of a car pulling up next to us brings me out of those memories, and I sit up.

"Nap over?" Sam asks.

"Yes," I say.

Having remembered all those moments, now I know why she was so angry. She had fallen in love with me, and I had sheltered her, and then I had run away.

"Good," she says. "Max is here."

That wasn't what I wanted to hear.

Because in those memories, I found something else, found something I had chosen to forget.

Those tender moments hadn't just made her fall in love with me, but they had also brought me to love her.

And I want to protect her again, just like Mary. Yet Max is here, and we're about to go back to Division Six where security will probably be much tighter, where Miss Tanaka will most assuredly be waiting, and maybe the CIA will also have their spies. We're going to go there and try to steal a substance that's probably worth more than any of us can imagine.

All because it's what Joe wanted, and what Taggart needs.

The side door opens, exposing us to the twilight sun, and Max climbs in, covered in blood.

CHAPTER 38

Max flops on the floor just after he enters, the blood on him smearing everything he touches.

As soon as she gets the outside door closed, Sam opens the divider door.

"Get moving! To the hospital!"

The van starts up, and George quickly puts it into motion.

Sam returns to check over Max. Mary also bends down over him. There's not enough room for me to be of any use, so I hang back and watch.

They roll him over onto his back. From where I sit, the slice to his stomach is obvious. His shirt gaps open where the blade had sliced him. His blood still runs from the cut.

"Steve, under the seat," Sam shouts.

I get up, shaky on my legs as the van takes a corner. I lift the seat and there's a first aid kit underneath.

A large one.

I pull it out and open it up.

I find a large number of rolled up gauze bandages. Sam seems to plan for everything. There's also a can of anti-bacterial spray.

While I've been getting the kit out, Sam ripped Max's shirt off him. The wound on his stomach looks dark and angry.

Sam has her hand out.

I hand her the spray.

She sprays the wound, drops the can, and sticks her hand back out.

I hand her the first roll of gauze.

She unrolls it and stuffs it on the wound, then sticks her hand back out. It's covered in Max's blood.

I hand her the next roll.

Mary props up Max's torso just enough so that Sam can wrap the bandage around him.

Two more rolls, and then I hand her the tape.

The blood probably still flows under all the gauze, and it's probably not going to stop without medical intervention, but maybe it'll keep him alive.

"Sam," Max says. His voice is weak.

"What happened?" she says.

"Won't make it to the hospital," he says. "Must tell you, they gave..."

His voice gives out, and he has to stop to take a few breaths.

"They gave what?" Sam asks.

"They gave it to him," Max says. "They're waiting for..."

He stops again.

"Gave it to who? What happened, Max?"

"Archon," he says after a moment.

"Archon? What's that mean?" Sam asks. "Did Archon do this to you, did Anna?"

Then he lifts his head.

"Dying," he says. "Take me, Steve."

He coughs. A bubble of blood escapes his lips.

Oh, shit.

He lays his head back down. His breathing has turned ragged.

"Max! Max!" Sam shakes him, but he's not responding. His chest is still moving, but he's not responsive.

Sam looks to me.

"I don't want to do this," I say. I don't want Max's memories.

"You have to, Steve. We have to know what happened."

Please, no.

But I know I have to.

We need it. Max knows we need it, and he's going to die anyway.

I had sworn not to take any more lives, but I keep doing it. First Joe, and now...

I leave my seat behind and crawl over to where Max is losing his battle to live. Mary moves out of the way so that I can sit in her spot.

The blood is all over.

I look at Max. His face is pale, his breath, shallow. The blood on his lips is proof he's going. His eyes are shut, lids fluttering just a little.

I still don't want to do it. I don't want his memories.

But Sam is right. We have to know.

I place my hand on Max's forehead, and his eyes open. He looks at me, nods.

Then I take everything he is from him.

CHAPTER 39

Having lost the CIA spooks in the maze underneath the freeway, I make my way back to the Division Six labs to complete my mission. I need to find out exactly who is at the lab, find out who is out looking for us, if they are even looking at all.

The building comes up on my right, shiny, silver, typical suburban city business complex. Four stories of offices that supposedly house construction companies, lawyers, importers, anything at all except its actual tenants.

Just the sight of it burns me up.

I pull into the front parking lot. A few of the cars are here, which means there are a dozen or more out looking for us. Good luck.

I drive down into the parking garage. Just a swing through to look and see, make sure they didn't park the cars down here just to lull us into thinking no one was home.

But the garage is mostly empty, too.

The only oddity is the medical van parked just outside the elevators.

I park the car, leave it running, just to take a look around.

I walk over to the van, look inside. No one's home.

I go around the back of it, pop open the doors, which are unlocked. Inside, it's just a medical van.

I hear a door open.

The stairs.

I turn around, and I'm staring at a man who's face I recognize, but he's older than I remember, with white hair that used to be salt and pepper, a crooked nose that, at one time, had far fewer pockmarks in it, and a jowly face that was once near free of wrinkles. But there's something about him, something vital, that I had never seen in him before, either.

It takes a long time before I realize the ultimate problem I have with seeing him here in the garage at the bottom of Division Six. The last I knew, he was dead.

"Hello, Max," he says.

"Brad," I say, tentatively.

"Nice of you to come by," he says.

"I thought you were dead," I say.

Brad Archon laughs with that half maniacal laugh that I remember. "Hardly," he says. "Just waiting."

"Waiting?" I ask.

"You know," he says, speaking as if I hadn't said a word, "it's a shame that your revitalization didn't work. You had such promise. Your skills were, well, something of a legend."

He takes a step toward me.

"Why did you leave us?"

"I couldn't take it," I say.

I couldn't take working with Joe any more, not after he ruined me. Funny how I ended up working with him, anyway.

"Your mind cracked," Brad says, "just like mine, or so I hear."

"Don't talk about that," I say.

The first ember of rage in me, the other that I can't control. I can't let him take over, now.

"Why not? I completely understand what you went through."

He takes another step toward me, but the rage is bubbling. I stand my ground.

"You understand nothing. You're crazier than I ever was." There it is.

"Ah, no. Now I am better. You see?"

He waves a hand, and the next thing I know, I'm flying through the air.

My back crashes up against something that feels like concrete, and then I fall to the asphalt below.

I don't feel any broken bones, but now I'm cursing Joe for even trying to cure me.

Get up. Get up.

Brad walks toward me, slow, deliberate.

"Why did you work so hard to stop us, Max?"

"You're spewing bullshit," I say as I get my feet under me. My back feels like it's broken, but it can't be, not if I can stand.

I reach for my gun. I should have had it out in the first place.

He lifts his hand, swipes through the air. My hand feels like it's been hit by an iron bar. The gun flies away to land a dozen feet off to my left.

"Oh really?" Brad asks. "I know how many of your kind you killed to keep them out of our hands."

It wasn't me, it was the rage. And Joe. He told me to. He had a plan.

"No one deserved to end up like Taggart, under your thumb for life," I say.

At the time, I hadn't realized it was his thumb. I thought it was Miss Tanaka's.

"On the contrary, it was our duty to bring them in, cure them. What happened to Taggart and you was . . . unfortunate."

"You..." I rush him.

He swings his arm again, only this time, there's a blade at the end of it. The line of fire it drags across my belly burns.

He steps out of the way, and I stumble past him, to land up against my car.

I scramble around to the driver's side. It's time to leave. The blood is already soaking my shirt.

I climb in, shut the door, put it in gear, and squeal the tires in my haste to leave.

Brad Archon stands there, watching me, letting me go.

Oh, tell your friends I'm waiting for them, Max, waiting to welcome them home.

CHAPTER 40

I come away from my contact with Max feeling energized, alive. I have his memories, all of them, and I'll need to sort through them, just like I have to finish sorting through Joe's, but that's for another day.

"We can't," I say, once I realize what Max's memory means for us.

"Can't what?" Sam asks.

"Can't go to Division Six," I say.

"We damned well can," Taggart says.

I look behind me, and he's got his head stuck through the doorway.

"No, no. We can't. Brad Archon is alive, and they've given him the cure."

Taggart looks confused.

"What's that mean?"

"It means that he can throw people around without touching them. It means that he can send people his thoughts."

"You know this?" Sam asks.

"He did it to Max," I say.

A hush falls over the van. Other than the road noise, it's silent.

It isn't long, though, before Taggart breaks the silence.

"It doesn't matter," he says. "I'll die soon if I don't go back."

Secretly, I wonder if he really will die, or if he'll just lose his reprieve from his disadvantages.

"They're waiting for us, expecting us, and now, Max is dead. We have one less person to help."

"What about Joe's plan?" Sam asks.

It's not what I hear, though. I hear, "What about me?"

And Sam is right.

I can't let her go the rest of her life without the cure. Unless we steal it, she'll be stuck, like she is now, in the dark.

"No," I say, "You're right. Max's memory was so strong, so fresh, it's hard…"

I hope they accept that explanation.

Taggart sighs.

"But, we need more help. Do you know anyone?"

I don't. I mostly stayed away from everyone.

"I'll help," George says from the cab.

"No," I say. "You keep Mary safe."

"I don't need to be kept safe, Steve," Mary says. "I can shoot, and you know it."

"We don't want to kill anyone," I say.

"I do," says Taggart as he looks at Max's corpse.

"So do I," says Sam, "and there are a couple others that will help."

"What about Max's body?" Mary asks.

Sam looks at Taggart.

"The cemetery," they say in unison.

Taggart ducks his head back up front and I can hear him instructing George on where to go.

Sam pulls a cell-phone from her pocket and starts dialing.

"Who are you calling?" I ask.

"Help," she says.

CHAPTER 41

We reach the cemetery just after dark.

It turns out it's not really a cemetery in the true sense of the word. It's a deep lake, far inside a suburban forest about forty-five minutes north of downtown. The lake exists in what was once an old rock quarry, long abandoned. Rusting equipment casts shadows, for those of us that can see them, under the light of the few stars that have emerged.

At least it's a clear night.

The three of us, Sam, Taggart, and I, haul Max's body to the edge of the lake. Mary chooses to stay in the van, and George stays with her.

Sam pulls a piece of cord from her pocket that she ties around Max's foot and then around a heavy stone. She balances him on the cliff edge, twenty feet above the water.

"Any words?" Sam asks as she stands at the edge next to Max's body. I think I see a tear in her eye, but I'm not certain.

"He was an asshole," Taggart says, "but I'll miss him. He didn't deserve what happened to him."

Sam looks at me, and I shake my head. I've got nothing.

Sam uses a foot to push Max's body over the edge.

The splash when he hits the water sounds loud in my ears.

After a moment, the stone has drawn him out of sight.

Back in the van, the floor is covered with his blood. Sam pulls a pair of towels out from under a seat, and we set to cleaning it up as best we can.

When we're done, we stuff the towels in a garbage bag and stow it under a seat.

"What now?" I ask.

"Tony, I think," she says. "He's closest. Then Amy."

"Are they like you?" Mary asks.

Sam nods.

I shudder at the idea of three people in the van who haven't been cured.

"Can you even get them into the van?" I ask.

"Yes," she says. "Not all of us are as sensitive as you."

"As I was," I say.

She sighs.

Taggart gives George instructions on how to find Tony, and then comes back to sit with us.

I can still smell Max's blood.

"What's the plan after we pick these two up," I ask, hoping to forget about the smell.

I'm assuming Sam has a plan. She's known Joe the longest of us, and I'm hoping he confided something in her, even though I'm guessing he didn't.

"You tell me," Sam says. "You're the one with the direct line to Joe and Max."

Right.

What was Joe's goal?

"Joe wanted three things," I say. "Keep Brad Archon from getting cured, disseminate the recipe or destroy it, and fix the two of you and anyone else we find. We've already failed the first one."

"You sure?" Taggart asks.

"Yes."

"Which means we need to get into the building, find the pre-made serum, get out, and burn the place to the ground," Sam says.

"I know where the serum is," Taggart says, "and I can get Miss Tanaka to give us the key."

"What about Brad Archon?" I ask. "My memories of what he did to Max are fresh. If he doesn't want you near him, you won't be able to get close."

"If we overwhelm him..."

"With three of us? You didn't see it," I say.

"He won't see me," Sam says.

"What if he does?" I ask. "I don't want you anywhere near him."

I'm feeling protective of her.

Mary looks my way. I can't read her face.

"You don't have a choice. You think he'll let you near him? Not a chance. He must know about what you can do. Anna would have told him. He won't let you within thirty feet if he knows you are there."

She has a point.

My outrage at Joe's betrayal rears its head again. If he hadn't sold me out to them... But then, I wouldn't be able to walk in the sunlight, either.

"All right," I say. "You win. Taggart and I will go after the serum. You keep an eye out for Brad. What can the others do?"

"Tony is all muscle, much like this guy," she says while poking Taggart in the shoulder.

"Hey," Taggart says.

"He can move things with his mind."

"Like Brad," I say.

"Right. Amy can affect electrical circuits, cause them to spike or shut them off. She'll go with you in case you need her to get through the lock."

"Why are we splitting up?" I ask.

"Two goals, two teams."

I catch Mary looking at me again.

"What about me?" she asks.

"You're staying in the van with George," I say.

"The hell I am. I can shoot. I'm going to help."

"We're not here to kill anyone," I say.

"You're not? What about Brad Archon?"

"No," I say.

Now Sam is looking at me.

"She has a point, Steve," Sam says.

"Fine, then George comes," I say. "Mary stays with the van."

I am *not* going to let her get hurt.

"Don't be ridiculous," Mary says. "George is not in any shape to do this kind of thing. If you have to run, he won't be able to keep up."

She's right, but I don't want to admit it. I don't like Sam going to face Brad Archon, and I certainly don't like Mary going inside the building at all.

"If I'd had my way, both you and George would be safe at home," I say. "In fact, we can drop you two off at a restaurant, give you some money, and you can catch a cab home."

Something snaps in Mary, and the fury erupts from every pore.

"God dammit, Steve, no wonder you spent thirty years alone! I loved you then, and I love you now, and I can understand why you are more interested in Sam. She's your kind, I get that. But I am *not* going to let you run me out of your life. You deserted me once. Not this time."

"Mary, I..."

She had seen it. She probably saw it before I ever noticed.

"Don't deny it, Steve. Ever since you saw her, you can't stop looking at her. There's something between you, and that's fine."

"There's nothing between us, now," says Sam.

I would have thought Sam would have better sense than to jump in to this.

"Not you, too, Sam. It's obvious to everyone. Even Taggart. I'm going. I'm going to help Sam kill that guy that did this to you all, and you're not going to stop me. You are not leaving me out of your life again."

When she stopped, we all sat in silence.

She had made me promise to take her before the end, and now, she was making me involve her in this fiasco we were about to embark upon. I do my best to avoid looking at Sam the entire time.

"Okay," I say, breaking the silence. "You go with Sam."

"Damn right I do."

CHAPTER 42

The silence in the van persists until Sam, apparently having made up her mind about something, moves to sit next to Mary.

At first, Mary seems a bit put off by it, but Sam whispers something into her ear that I don't quite catch because of the road noise, and Mary relaxes.

After a few moments, they start talking between themselves, and throwing glances my way.

I contemplate pretending to sleep again and slipping into Sam's head, but decide against it. It might be better that I don't know what they are talking about.

An hour later, George pulls up to a run-down apartment building, and Taggart jumps out.

When he returns, he's got a man with him that's even bigger than Taggart is.

"I'm Tony," he says as he enters the van and flexes his arm. "Taggart says you need some muscle."

I laugh, and I don't know why. It wasn't very funny. He grins with a goofy, lopsided effort, and sits down.

Tony has a tattoo of Popeye on the bicep that he flexed. Shows our age, I guess, and perhaps a bit of his humor. I wonder if he eats spinach. As goofy as his smile is, the rest of him is pure bruiser. I doubt he eats vegetables at all.

He may not be as sensitive as I was to the pheromone that we put off, but I notice that he sits as far as he can from Sam. Far better than I would have accomplished. I would never have gotten near the van.

Twenty minutes later, the van comes to a stop and Taggart gets out again. Outside the van, it's dark, and I can't see where we are, exactly.

When he returns, he has a cute, short blonde on his arm. She looks a bit like an elf. So damned thin she could be a stand-in for a light pole.

But the thing I notice most about her is her smell. It's intoxicating. I breathe deep, then realize what I'm doing.

I look around the van to see if anyone else is doing the same, but they're not. Sam looks at Amy, waves, but doesn't seem to have much of a reaction. Tony, however, seems to be trying to hold his breath. Her pheromones obviously bother him.

Amy notices this, and makes her way to the back of the van. I find myself wanting to follow her. What the hell is this?

I mean, obviously, Joe's serum affected the way I react to the pheromones put off by others like me. I hardly even notice Tony, though I realize now that I could probably recognize him anywhere just by his scent. Sam, I notice easily, and she smells good. I know that it's affecting how much I like her, how much I want to be next to her.

But Amy? Amy's pheromones are like heroine. One whiff, and I'm addicted. I want more. I want to move and sit closer to her, right next to her. I want to possess her.

But I don't. I don't know anything about her except what she smells like.

"Steve," I hear Sam say. "Everything okay?"

"What?"

I look Sam's way. Both her and Mary are looking at me, sharing the same look that borders on disgust. I realize then that I was staring at Amy.

"Are you all right? You seem distracted."

"Yeah, I'm fine," I say.

And it is a little better. Not looking at her helps, but it's not quite enough.

I need to get out of here.

I start to get up.

"Where are you going?" Sam asks.

"Up front. I want to talk to George." It's a good excuse.

"We need to discuss the operation," Sam says.

"We already discussed it, didn't we?" I need to get out of here, shut that door, turn on the air conditioning. "You and Mary and Tony go after Brad, Taggart and I go after the serum."

"Taggart, you, and Amy," Sam corrects me.

"That's what I said," I say.

If I don't get out now...

"You haven't even introduced yourself to her," Sam says.

Right. Like I want to do that.

"I'm Amy," she says, sticking her hand out.

Oh God. I can't. I keep my hands where they are, one on the seat next to me, one on the roof, holding me steady.

Amy smiles at me, but it's a tentative smile, like she's unsure of what's going on. I'm sure as hell not sure what's going on, but I fear what touching her might do.

I had thought I was falling in love with Sam. I had thought that's what it was, that her pheromones were just an incentive. We had a history together. But here, confronted with Amy, whose presence wants to rewire every thought I had about possible futures I would have with Sam, I am terribly aware that I no longer know if what I feel for Sam is love, or if it's something else.

"C'mon Steve, quit being rude," Mary says.

Maybe, maybe...

I take my hand from the roof of the van, extend it. She takes my hand. We shake.

I don't know what I was expecting. There's no jolt of electricity, no lightning strike. It's just a hand, but my brain is still wild with desire for her.

"Nice to meet you," I say.

And then I force myself to let go, and I rush past Taggart as he's closing the side door behind him. I slip through the barrier door and into the passenger seat, pulling the door shut behind me.

I roll down the window, take a few breaths. The desire for Amy fades, but it's not going to go away quickly.

"What are you doing up here?" George asks.

"I needed some air."

And then, for the first time, I realize what her scent reminds me of. She smells like berries, just like the scent that almost got me caught by Division Six.

And she's going to be on my team.

MINDERS

I close my eyes and take another deep breath of the outside air as if it's the last breath I'll ever get.

CHAPTER 43

The lights of the city flash by as George drives us to our destination. It's beautiful in a way that I hadn't realized when I could only look at the night sky and hate it for limiting me.

Amy's scent seeps through the door, but the open window and the breeze that blows through it helps to dissipate it enough that it doesn't fill me with desire. I can stand it.

But once we get started?

"What the hell do I do, George?"

We haven't talked much since we were taken from his house. There hasn't been the time or the opportunity.

"With the girls?"

My chuckle is unexpected amidst all my tension. "Yeah, with the girls, only now, there's a third."

He looks at me, lifts an eye.

I guess I had better explain.

"The cure Joe injected me with, it's hardly a cure," I say. "It's just another modification. Sure, I can go out in the sunlight, now, and it gave me the one new ability, maybe more."

"More?" he asks.

"Possibly, And there's something else."

He switches lanes to get around a slowpoke early seventies Volkswagen Beetle that's spewing smoke out the exhaust.

"And it has to do with the girls?" he says.

"Well, do you remember me telling you how I couldn't stand the smell of others of my kind?"

"Yeah," he said.

"Now, well, it's different." I stick my hand out the window like a wing, let the air move it up and down like I used to do as a kid.

"Tell me," he says.

"Well, I've always had a place in my heart for Mary, loved her, I thought. And then Sam came around. She smelled good. She smells good. I can't keep her out of my head most of the time. I thought I was falling in love with her. I mean, we had a history long ago, and I thought it was just us getting back together, resuming that old romance."

"But?"

"But then we pick up Amy and I can't keep my eyes off her. Sam is hardly noticeable, anymore."

"And how is that related to the way she smells?"

"It's a pheromone," I say. "And she's got a lot of it. It's the same one that drove us away from each other, before, but now, for me, it's like a drug. I have to have more of it. Even now, the only thing that keeps me from going back there and hitting on her is that I know it's just that pheromone causing me to do it."

"She *is* cute," George says.

"Shut up. I'm serious."

George laughs. "I know you're serious. I just wonder, with all that's going on, if you're not just worn out and need a rest."

"Maybe."

But I don't feel like I need a rest. I feel energized.

"So, what is your real problem?"

"I'm worried about what Sam will do," I say. "What if I can't control myself? What if I can't keep my mind on our task? This could screw it all up."

"How?"

"Amy's going to be on *my* team."

George laughs again, this time, big and loud. It takes him more than a minute to get it under control.

"Don't laugh," I say. "It's not at all funny."

"Probably not," he says with a smirk, "but with all the other trouble going on, you've got girl problems. It's funny."

"Only to an ex-cop."

"All right, you want my advice?" he asks.

"If you've got any worth sharing," I say.

"Put it out of your head until tomorrow. Worry about how you're going to get out of this place alive, tonight."

He's right.

"If only it was so easy," I say.

"Did I ever tell you why you had to save me that day?"

I bring my arm back in from outside and turn to face him. All the earlier mirth is gone from his face.

"I don't think so."

"I was distracted. My wife and I had an argument that morning, and I couldn't keep it out of my head. I kept the argument going, even though she wasn't there, instead of concentrating on my job. If I had been paying attention, I would have heard that guy, and he wouldn't have got the drop on me.

"Don't be me. Go back there, get used to it so that it's not bugging you the whole time you're inside. If you can't handle it, you'll put everyone at risk."

The wind blowing into the cab of the van seems to be getting colder. I roll up the window.

"You're right," I say. "I just don't know..."

"Look. At the very least, you have to tell them."

"You think so?"

"Yeah, I do."

"That will be awkward," I say.

"More awkward than explaining why their dead?"

He has a point.

I put my hand to the door and take a deep breath. Maybe I can just hold my breath the whole time.

Right.

CHAPTER 44

"**Y**ou what?" Sam asks.

She's at the far end of the van with Amy and Mary, while Tony and I sit as close to the bulkhead as we can, as far away from them as possible. In the closed confines, it doesn't seem to be helping at all.

Taggart sits, in the middle, laughing.

"I said I don't think it's a good idea for Amy to be on my team."

I try to keep my eyes on Sam and Mary and away from Amy. It's far too difficult. What the hell was George thinking? I'll never be able to overcome her in time. Ignoring her is like ignoring the rattlesnake that just bit you on the leg. Never going to happen.

"I heard that. What I didn't hear is why," she says.

"I can smell her," I say, leaving it as vague as possible.

"What the hell are you talking about. You're sitting right next to Tony," she says. "I thought you said the cure fixed that problem. It did for Taggart."

"I thought it did," I say. "But..."

"Quit being evasive," she says. "We're running out of time."

She's right. We are running out of time. We'll arrive at the Division Six any minute.

"All right. You know how some animals are attracted to others just because of their pheromones? And remember how Joe said our pheromones drove each other away?"

"Sure," she says. She has a skeptical look on her face. I deliberately avoid looking at Amy.

"Joe didn't cure me," I say. "He changed me—again. And now, the pheromones you two give off attract me."

Taggart busts out laughing.

Mary looks confused.

Sam's face is blank.

"I thought, you know, that I was falling for you again," I say, knowing I'm screwing it up badly, but I can't think of any other way to tell it all in the time we have. "But when Amy came in, the smell of her was overwhelming. It *is* overwhelming, completely distracting. It's difficult to think of anything else."

Now Mary looks crushed, but she knew it was happening. She knew I was falling for Sam again. But Sam's face is covered with so many conflicting emotions, I can't tease them apart. It's as effective a defense at figuring out what she's thinking as a stone blank face would be.

Amy shifts just a little, enough so that I can see her out of the corner of my eye.

I shift my eyes. I can't look. I won't be able to resist. I almost can't resist, now.

Sam's face sets, blank again.

"Tony," she says, "go up front."

I look at Tony. His goofy grin is still on his face, but I can see he feels a little grateful for the order to leave. He probably wants to leave the stench that I am drowning in. The stench that I can no longer get enough of.

When the door shuts, Sam strides the length of the van and sits down next to me.

"You need her," she says in a quiet voice. "If Anna isn't there or you can't get the key from her, Amy may be able to trick the locks somehow."

"I just don't know if I can put it out of my mind," I say.

"Would a gas mask help?" she asks.

"A gas mask?"

"Yeah, there are a couple under the seats, in case Div Six ever tried to teargas us or something."

Inadvertently, my eyes shift and I catch sight of Amy. She's so beautiful, sitting on her hands, talking with Mary and trying to avoid looking like she's listening, though I know she can hear every word we say.

I tear my eyes away, stare at Taggart.

"It might," I say. At this point, I'll try anything.

"Stand up."

I stand and Sam lifts up the seat. While she rummages around, I stare at Taggart. He's still chuckling to himself. He can hear everything we're saying, too, but he's not going to pretend he isn't. I notice one other thing about him that I hadn't seen before. His skin is turning pale. The veins on his neck stand out, light purple streaks, that weren't there before.

"Taggart's veins," I whisper.

He looks up at me.

The seat slams shut, and I look away from him and sit down.

Sam holds a gas mask that looks like it's rated for bio-hazard duty.

I take it from her, struggle to find the straps and figure out how it goes on.

"Here," she says, putting her hands into the mess I've made of it. Our fingers touch. For that moment, my awareness of Amy fades. Then Sam pulls her fingers away and Amy's presence is back, full force.

Sam slips the mask over my head, adjusts the straps.

"Breathe," she says.

I realize I had been holding my breath.

I breathe.

The first few breaths, I can still smell her, but soon after, her scent and the pheromones in it rapidly diminish.

I feel like a fool with this on, but it helps, better even than being up in the cab.

Then I notice something else is missing. I can't smell Sam, either, and I miss it.

"Better?" she asks.

"Yes," I say.

I look at Amy. She's cute, and still chatting with Mary. Without her pheromones pushing at me, I'm still attracted to her, but it's no longer the need, it's no longer something I have to fight.

Now, I can think about other things, like Taggart and his veins.

"Is Taggart all right?" I ask.

Sam looks at Taggart, and grimaces.

"He's fine for another few hours," she says.

"How did that come on so fast?" I ask.

"It always does that," she says.

"I hear you talking about me," Taggart grumbles.

"Sorry," I say, "I just... Can you do this?"

"Yeah, I'm fine."

He gets up and moves away from us, and sits down next to Amy. She smiles, reaches up and ruffles his hair.

"So," Sam says, "since we can't talk about him, why don't you tell me why you think you're falling for me, and why you think I'd be interested in the first place."

"I don't..."

The bulkhead door flings open as the van rolls over a speed bump, interrupting me.

"We're here," Tony shouts through the door.

Sam smiles at me. "I guess it'll have to wait."

The front of the van dips and I look through the door and out the front windshield. Down into the garage where I worry Brad Archon is waiting for us. Him, or an army of Division Six.

CHAPTER 45

George brings the van to a halt, while Sam and Taggart are flinging up the seats. She's got a cache of weapons beneath them, pistols, shotguns, a couple semi-automatics. Nothing I feel comfortable using.

"The place looks deserted," George says.

"Deserted?" Sam asks.

"Yeah, no cars anywhere. Not even outside."

A setup?

Crap.

"We go look, anyway," Sam says. "Taggart doesn't have long."

Deserted. It's not here.

"Sam," I say, Max's memory of his encounter with Brad Archon still fresh in my head, "if Brad could get into Max's head to say something to him..."

She catches where I was going.

"...then he might have been able to learn what we were planning from him," she finishes.

"Let me look," I say.

She nods.

"Do it quick. Taggart, Tony and I will scout."

They each grab a gun, then swing open the door of the van. The garage *is* empty. The lights are still on, but it feels abandoned, anyway.

I sit down on a seat. Mary comes over to me and sits by me.

"I'll watch him," she says. She has a pistol on her lap.

I lean back. I close my eyes.

This is going to be hard. The adrenaline of arriving, expecting to find opposition, the excitement and headiness of Amy, all has my emotions raised to a level that will make it difficult to concentrate on something so ephemeral as the thoughts of someone else.

Think about need again. Breathe slow. Breathe deep.

My heart pumps at the same steady beat. I still don't know how that works. Joe never explained it to me. I wonder if he can. But everything else in me remains wired, ready to burst into action.

And action is not what I need now.

No.

I need to think about the serum. The cure. Look at it.

My vision shifts.

I'm in a lab. Microscopes, refrigerators, chemicals, centrifuges. I look down at my hands.

I don't know what I expected to see, but I had hoped to find Miss Tanaka. But these hands aren't hers. They are an old man's hands.

I feel you, there inside me.

Shit.

We're not so different, you and I. Joe's serum works wonders, does it not?

Can you hear me?

Of course I can, just as you can hear me.

Are you...

You don't have to ask. You know who I am.

Brad Archon.

Good. Your friend Max gave up your whole plan without even knowing.

Where are you?

Oh, let's not discuss that yet. I want to know, how's Taggart doing?

He needs the serum.

I'm not inclined to give it to him. He and his friends nearly succeeded in keeping me from receiving its wonderful benefits.

Please. He'll die without it.

I intend him to. Him and the others that betrayed me, lied to me, hid the side-effects from me. I paid millions, and all they sold me was something that didn't work. It almost killed me, you know.

I know.

But I'm not dead, and now I'll live for as long as I wish. Look at my hands. Even now, the age is leaving them, the cells are repairing themselves. I'll look as young as you do in less than a year. And you know what? That's only the beginning.

What do you mean?

With people like you working for me, people I can trust, I'll have control of every major corporation on the planet.

I'm not working with you.

Oh, you will, when you understand what I have to offer.

What about the government?

Oh, you mean that deal with the CIA? As soon as I recovered my faculties, I quashed that deal. The government is small potatoes, and the deal happened because I had people with small minds in place. But you, you are like me.

I'm not at all like you.

Oh, but you are. You have the memories of a thousand people in your head. I can feel them, waiting there in case you ever need them. You do what you have to so that you survive. You are a winner, Steve. I know you'll deny it, but I can feel it in you. It was those fools who left you damaged. Now, you are complete, the way you should have been. It's time to pay them back.

You can't offer me enough.

How about the lives of your friends, the ones that are out there, poking around right now.

He looks at a monitor, and I can see them in it, and just in the edge of the camera's view, a blinking light.

A bomb?

Yes. A bomb. That whole place is rigged to explode. We'll call it an industrial accident. The building doesn't cost much in the scheme of things. It won't be looked into beyond the nightly news, because no one will die, officially.

How will you be able to trust me if you put me over this barrel?

Because you and I are special, Steve. I can always be there, right in your head.

I agree.

I don't have much choice, not right now. Not while Sam is standing right under that bomb.

Good choice. Now, here's what I want you to do, and know this: I'll be watching.

CHAPTER 46

Brad's instructions are clear. What's also clear is that he needs an arch-villain name and a superhero to stop him. He's not all-powerful, but his ability to move things and his ability to get into peoples' heads, talk to them, hear what they're thinking—that makes him close to all powerful.

And when the vision shifts back, I can still feel him there, watching. He can do it while he's awake, lucid, walking around. Me, I'm dizzy again.

And I'm at a loss as to how to avoid doing what he wants.

"Mary," I say when I can sit up. "Get them back in here."

She looks at me for a moment, as if she has a question, and then she exits the van in search of them. If I could do what Brad could do, we wouldn't need radios or anything, but right now...

Gah, thirty years of being solo and out of the world leaves me slow, sometimes.

I shout out the still open door. "Mary, come back!"

"Amy, do you have a cell phone?"

"Yeah," she says.

"And Sam's number? Or Tony's?"

"Right," she says, understanding where I'm going with it. "Are you all right?"

"Fine. Just a bit dizzy. It'll pass."

She pulls out her phone and starts dialing.

I spend the next few minutes, while waiting for the others to come back, trying to figure a way out of this mess, but I know he's listening in. I finally close my eyes and stare at the inside of my eyelids.

By the time they return, I've recovered my equilibrium.

"George, get us out of the garage, then stop at the parking lot entrance."

The van lurches into motion.

"What are we doing back here?" Sam asks.

"None of what we need is here," I say. "It's at Mr. Archon's personal compound." That's one of the things he admonished me to do: call him Mr. Archon.

"Wonderful," says Sam.

The van comes to a stop.

"Okay. George, Mary, Taggart, get out."

"What?" Taggart and Sam ask at the same time.

"You can't be serious," Mary says.

"I'm serious. I don't have much time to explain, but here's the short version. Mr. Archon doesn't want you three, and he's willing to let you go. He has eyes on this van," I'm reluctant to say how, "and he will kill us all if we don't do as he says."

"How do you know this?" George asks.

"I talked to him."

Gasps of disbelief come from almost everyone.

"How?" Sam asks.

"I found him, he found me? I'm not sure. He told me he'll give us the serum if I do what he asks."

"What's that?"

"He wants me to work for him."

"You're not seriously considering that after what he did to Max, are you?" Sam asks. She looks like she's ready to kill me now.

"I don't see that I have a choice," I say.

"Why?"

"Because he has bombs set in that building, and he's watching us right now. If we don't do what he asks, he'll destroy the building, send the video of our van entering and leaving to the FBI with the photos of you and the weapons you were carrying."

"He can't do that," George says. "It'll expose what Archon Global has done to all of you."

"No it won't. We're terrorists. He says he can ensure that it ends in a firefight and that we all end up dead.

"Please. We don't have another choice."

"You'll all be safe?" George asks.

"He assured me of it."

"What about me," Taggart asks. He's looking worse than just a few minutes ago. He doesn't have a lot of time left.

"He blames you, along with Max and Joe, for putting him in this bind, for interfering."

"Why not Sam?"

"She stays alive as long as I keep him happy."

Sam inhales sharply. Now she knows why I'm doing this. I would have liked to lie, but I couldn't come up with a good one.

"It'll kill him," Sam says.

"That's Mr. Archon's intent."

"Why do you keep calling him Mr. . . . He's in your head," Sam says, figuring it out.

"Yes."

She turns to Taggart.

"Out," she says. "Stay where we can find you."

And then she remembers that Mr. Archon can hear her.

"I'm sorry," she says, and gives him a hug.

Taggart looks at me, and I expect a hurt look, but his look is sympathetic. He's been where I am, beholden to something he hates just to stay alive.

"Keep her safe, Steve," Taggart says.

"I will."

He pulls open the door and exits.

George exits from the driver's door and then pokes his head into the side doorway.

Mary gets up, comes to me, lifts the gas mask. Amy's scent overwhelms me immediately, but Mary puts her mouth over mine, and kisses me like it was thirty years ago. For that moment, all I can smell is her.

She backs away from me, puts the mask back down, wipes her lips.

"Keep yourself safe, too. Don't forget your promise to me. I want you to remember me forever."

"I won't forget."

She steps out of the van, and then George shuts the door.

"What now?" Sam asks.

"You and me, up in the cab. Tony and Amy back here."

"I have to be in the cab? What if the sun..."

"The sun won't be up for hours, still. We'll be there before sunrise. And he wants to know you're with me. Also, I haven't driven anything in thirty years."

"This sucks, you know," she says.

"It could be worse."

"Worse?"

An enormous roar rocks the van, and then a shock-wave hits and the van rocks underneath us.

We both scramble up to the front and look out the windows.

Behind us, the building has exploded and collapsed. A giant, fire-lit dust cloud comes our way and envelopes the van.

Through the dust, I can see George, Mary and Taggart, all on the ground. They're moving, though, not dead.

"What the hell?" Sam asks.

"I think that's his way of saying, 'Get moving'."

Sam grimaces, then buckles up.

We drive away, leaving our three friends on the side of the road.

I hope they can get away before the authorities show up.

CHAPTER 47

Mr. Archon's compound sits on a private lake that's roughly two hour's drive to the east, hidden on the eastern slopes of the Cascade mountains. I don't know how he got out there so fast, how they got that building cleared so quickly and the bombs planted. I can only guess he'd been planning the destruction of the building for some time.

Which might mean he's been in control for a lot longer than I thought.

I sit quietly while Sam drives. I don't have anything much to say to her, and anything I would want to say to her, I don't want Mr. Archon to hear. I don't even want to think for fear of him listening in, but it's hard to stop thinking.

At least I don't have to wear the damned gas mask up here.

She doesn't say a word for a half-hour or more, other than to ask for directions. I know she's mourning for Taggart and Max. Max is already dead, and Taggart might as well be. There's little chance of returning in time to administer the cure to him. Having him get out of the van killed him.

"What happens when we get there," Sam asks.

"I can only guess," I say.

She glances at me. Lines of worry cross her forehead. "Then guess."

"The three of you get the treatment, and the binder."

She glances at me again. She knows what it means. The four of us will be Mr. Archon's slaves until we die, which could be a very, very long time.

"There's got to be a way," she says.

There would be, if I could figure out how to kick him out of my head.

I lean back in my seat, put my head back.

"What are you doing?" Sam asks.

"Resting," I say.

I'm trying not to think about what I'm doing. I'm hoping that, even though he's in my head, he's not paying attention the whole time, that he's not listening to my every thought.

If I could just wall him off.

Don't do that, Steve.

Will you ever leave my head?

As soon as I'm sure I've got you working for me. You've done well so far, don't screw it up.

Right.

I close my eyes and let my mind wander in darkness. Think about nothing. That's a hard thing to do, thinking about nothing. You end up thinking about thinking.

After a time, my ears start to feel the pressure changes. We're entering the mountains. I resist looking. I haven't seen them in anything but pictures for years, since I was a kid out skiing with my parents.

What I wouldn't give to see my parents again, right now.

I wouldn't even know where to begin to find them. I lost track of them right after the change, after I went underground, hid from the world.

No, wait. I didn't lose track of them.

The memory floods back into me.

The way my mom looked as I touched her arm that morning, her hair a mess because she had yet to prep herself for the day, still dressed in her nightgown.

She walks over to me.

"Are you all right, Stevie? You look pale."

"I'm fine Mom," I say.

She puts the back of her hand to my forehead like I'm twelve, still.

I reach up, take her by the wrist, and it happens.

I take everything, and I can't stop.

My eyes open. I haven't thought of that in so long, it's possible I locked it away before I met Sam for the first time. But the memory, now unlocked, is as fresh as if it happened yesterday.

"My mom was my first," I say to Sam.

"What?" she asks.

The moon reflects off the piles of snow that still dot the sides of the road. The darkness of the mountains rise up on either side of us, closing us in. If it were not for the other vehicles on the road, it would seem otherworldly.

"My mom. She was the first person I killed with my ability."

"Oh, Steve," she says. Her tone drips with sympathy. "Why didn't you tell me before?"

"I didn't remember. I had locked it away."

"Locked it away?"

"Yeah. I do that, sometimes. I hide the things I don't want to remember behind walls, and I lock them up. I did that with you."

"With me? Why?"

"I didn't want to remember."

"I understand that," she says. "Why didn't you want to remember? Was I that bad?"

I hear the joke. She's trying to make this easier, but I can't laugh.

"No," I say. "You were perfect."

"Then why?"

Sometimes, I don't make connections very quickly between the things that happen and the reasons I did them. Mom, she was an accident. My dad, he died because of my anger, because of his anger, because he wouldn't leave me alone about Mom.

"I almost killed you," I say. "Like I did my mom. I didn't want to remember killing my mom, and remembering what I almost did to you opened that door to my memories of my mom."

"So you locked them all away," Sam says.

"I did."

"You could have told me," she says. "You didn't have to leave."

"I couldn't trust myself," I say. "You were so vulnerable then. I had saved you, and then I almost killed you myself. I couldn't let that happen."

MINDERS

She puts her hand out across the void between us, puts her hand reassuringly on my leg. She doesn't say anything. She doesn't have to.

CHAPTER 48

A large metal gate blocks the entrance to a small canyon. A stream, glinting in the moonlight, flows out of that canyon along the side of the road. There's a phone box on the side of the road.

Sam rolls the window down to pick it up, but the gate starts opening before she can reach it.

"That's right," she says. "In your head."

I say nothing.

I open the door to the back, and Amy's scent wafts through into the cabin, making it hard for me to concentrate.

Tony still sits toward the front, Amy all the way at the back.

"We're here," I say.

"What happens next?" Amy asks.

Tony seems to have gone mute. He hasn't asked a question since the explosion.

"I'm not sure, but I think you'll be given the cure. You'll be able to walk in the sunlight again."

"There's a catch, isn't there?"

"Yes," I say. "You'll be forced to work for him."

"He can't make me do that," she says. "I'll leave."

"You won't be able to do that."

"Like Taggart," Tony says, breaking his silence.

"Yes."

Amy's fists clench the seat, her knuckles go white. I can tell she's trying to maintain her calm. Her pheromones incite me to leave my seat, go to her side, and comfort her.

But I can't do that.

Mr. Archon wants me up front.

I shut the door, roll down my window. Her scent and her pheromones rapidly diminish.

"Next time, *you* talk to them," I say.

"I'm driving," Sam says.

The road, more of a wide driveway, follows the stream up the canyon for about three miles until it rides a lip up and out of the canyon. At the crest, we can see the lake the stream feeds through the pine trees. It glitters under the star light.

Giant stone hills, nearly walls, bound the lake on three sides. It's as isolated as it can get. What I would give to spend a week floating on that lake under the sun.

Work for me faithfully, and you'll get your chance.

He knows how to ruin a moment.

The road circles around the lake for a quarter mile or so until we see lights through the trees.

Sam directs us around one last corner, and the drive opens up into a clearing in the forest that's dominated by a house built of stone, cedar, and what seems like a hundred thousand windows. Lights come on as the van follows the curve of the driveway, which leads us to park right in front of the door, as if it were a hotel.

But it's no hotel. There's no usher to greet us.

Instead, there are two armed men waiting for us. My guess is that they're Mr. Archon's personal bodyguards.

Good guess. Now come inside.

Sam shuts off the van, leaves the keys in the ignition.

I get out my side, which is the same side where the goons are standing.

"Hello," I say.

"Mr. Archon wants you all inside," says the one on the left. He's nearly identical to the one on the right. They're both big, muscular men with low brows and a number two haircut. Tony could probably take one of them. I doubt the rest of us could take the other.

Don't even think about it.

Get out of my head!

When we're done here, I'll leave you to your work. Until then...

You're not leaving.

Sam, Amy, and Tony step around the front of the van. I probably should have left the gas mask on, but outside the confines of the van, Amy doesn't affect me quite as much. I can still think.

To be sure, I take Sam's arm and put her between me and Amy.

It helps. Even though Sam's scent is not as strong, touching her keeps me grounded.

Together, we walk between the goons and up the tiled steps. The doors open, but I don't think they're automatic.

Mr. Archon is showing off.

We step through into a gigantic foyer. A staircase runs up the left side, carved mahogany railing and all. The right side of the room is dominated by a large painting of the Archon Global founder in his early days.

Once we are all in, the doors shut behind us.

A man walks through a doorway at the back. He's somewhat shorter than I expect, but not really short at all. Just the images I had from Max's memories made him seem so much larger. His hair is still white, but I can see, just under it, the dark color of fresh, young hair. The lines on his face are not as deep as I expect for a man that's seen more than eighty years. But I know that, having seen his hands. In a couple days, except for the bits of him that need to grow out, like his hair, he will be as young looking as the rest of us.

"Welcome," he says in a big, booming voice.

He smiles the smile of the young man in the painting. I can see immediately how he turned this company into the global power that it became. He commands the room.

So much so, that I almost don't notice Miss Tanaka enter the room behind him. But Mr. Archon's attention is distracted almost immediately, which allows me to break free of his gaze for just a moment, long enough to see her.

"Well," Mr. Archon says as he strides toward us, "I can see Steve's problem."

He doesn't get within reach of me, though. He looks right past Sam and I.

"Come here, Amy," he says. "I must absolutely see you."

Amy's pheromones.

Amy steps forward, hesitantly.

"Come, come. I won't hurt you. You'll see. I'm going to give you the world. I'm going to give it to you all."

Amy comes to a stop in front of him when he puts his hand out. I expected to see her tremble, but she's not trembling.

"Ah," Mr. Archon says. "Careful, but not frightened. I like that. If you do what I ask, none of you have any reason to be frightened."

"We don't?"

"No. You'll be able to go out into the world, do things you haven't done in thirty years. You'll have to work for me, of course, but that will hardly be a hardship."

"What if we don't want to work for you?" Sam asks.

Mr. Archon doesn't look up from Amy.

"Why wouldn't you want to work for me? Great pay, better benefits, a real life back, no more hiding."

"I don't want to spend my life working for the man who killed my friends," Sam says.

Mr. Archon looks up sharply, stamps his foot like a petulant child. His eyes look strangely unfocused despite his intense stare. "Quiet! I did no such thing. They got what they deserved for trying to stop me. You, my dear, only live because I like your boyfriend here, and I want him to be happy."

And then he returns his attention to Amy, almost as if nothing had happened.

"You," he says, lifting his finger to Amy's throat and then sliding it up to her chin until he pushes her head up so that she has to look into his eyes. "You will be mine."

The cure didn't fix his crazy.

"Mr. Archon," Miss Tanaka says. "They are ready."

"Good, good." He looks up, smiles, then claps. "Time to make you whole again!"

Sam looks at me. She's got fear in her eyes. "Don't worry," I say. "It'll be fine."

Fine, except for the binder.

"Yes, it'll be just fine," says Mr. Archon. "Go with Miss Tanaka, please."

"Come this way," Miss Tanaka says, motioning with her blood red fingernails.

We all start walking toward her, when something stops me cold and I can't move any further. Sam's hand slips from mine. There's nothing holding me, though. It's Mr. Archon.

"Not you, Steve. You and I need to talk."

Sam looks at me, worried, but I motion her to go.

She turns and follows the others, who have passed her by, but she keeps looking back my way until she enters the hallway and the door shuts behind her.

I'm not sure what to think. She won't be the same the next time I see her.

CHAPTER 49

"Come with me, Steve. Let's have a drink while we wait for our girls."

He almost sounds like he's trying to be my friend, like he's not about to enslave me forever, like he thinks he's doing me, and the rest of us, a favor.

I go with him, though. I need a way to distract him, and maybe if he has a drink or two...

"You keep scheming, Steve. I like that about you. Whatever you come up with, though, it won't work. In a few hours, we'll all be one happy family, and we can go about giving the world the Archon Global of the future."

"Of the future?"

"I already told you. Me, you, the others like us. We are the future of the human race. We shall lead the world to a better place."

Why is it that guys like this always want to rule the world?

"Oh, I don't want to rule the world, Steve. I want to own it."

He takes me down a hallway that opens into an opulent sitting room. Gold lighting fixtures, chairs that look for all the world like they came from the treasure hoard of a dragon. There's a fireplace along one wall that's got an opening as tall as I am. Every table looks to be hand-crafted from the most expensive wood Mr. Archon was able to lay his hands on.

There's a wet bar in one corner of the room made of black glass. He leads me over to it.

"What do you drink?" he asks.

"Water," I say. Anything else is a waste.

"C'mon, you've gotta have something with a little bite," he says.

"It doesn't affect me, and I don't like the taste, anyway," I say.

"Now that's interesting," he says. "It's amazing how that drug worked on you. For me, it hardly did anything except give me the ability to listen in on what people were thinking."

He pulls a bottle off the wall behind him. I don't get a good look at what it is. I'm watching him, waiting for my chance, if I have one.

"You want to know something?" he asks.

"Sure," I say.

He pours a couple fingers of his liquor into the bottom of a glass, over a couple cubes of ice. It's got a nice amber color. A whiskey perhaps.

"They say I went crazy. I didn't go crazy. It was all the whispering in my head. I couldn't control it. People thinking this or that, thinking thoughts about me they shouldn't be thinking. A *mess* I tell you."

"The treatment fixed that?"

He smiles.

"It did. And just like you, it gave me these new abilities. I can talk back, as you know. I can move whatever I wish. Nothing can hurt me, anymore."

He sets the glass on the bar in front of me.

"Drink!" he says, laughing.

I don't want to.

Drink, Steve.

The voice in my head is far more ominous.

I pick up the glass. It won't matter. It won't affect me at all.

I put the glass to my lips, take a sip.

It's smooth, doesn't burn like I expect.

I sip a little more. I can drink this.

"Good, yes?"

"It *is* good," I say.

"Now, we'll see if it doesn't make you feel a little more relaxed. You need to stop thinking of me as your enemy, Steve. I'm not your enemy. They are."

He sweeps his hand out in front of him, indicating everything outside his window.

"Everyone that ever kept you down, everyone that treated you poorly because you were different from them. Even that hack of a scientist Joe. He treated you, treated us, like a science experiment. You were no more important to him than a lab rat."

"Joe was my friend."

"Was he? Didn't he lie to you the whole time? He lied to me. He kept telling me the solution was just around the corner. And when he had it, he tried to keep it from me.

"He wasn't your friend, Steve. Friends don't treat friends that way.

"Me," he says, and looks straight at me. "Me, I'm your best friend, Steve."

"Then let us go," I say. "Give them the treatment. Don't use the binder. Let them make their own choices. Let me make my own choice."

Mr. Archon pours himself his own glass, over ice, just like the one he poured me. While he pours, silence hangs between us. I begin to worry that I've angered him.

"No, no. You haven't angered me. You haven't betrayed me, not like the others.

"I understand what you're saying, too. Trust me, I do. In a perfect world, I could do what you say, but these gifts of ours, the ones your friends have, the ones they will have, I can't just let them run free."

He steps out from behind the bar.

"Do you know how much it cost me to make these gifts, Steve?"

He puts his hand on my shoulder.

Don't you even think it.

"Billions. Billions! But we've remade humanity, at least for a few of us, and it was worth it. Imagine if word got out. Imagine if people could use their gifts in the light of day and everyone could see."

"You'd sell a lot of that treatment," I say.

He looks at me and smiles. The hand on my shoulder flexes.

"Yes, yes we would. But you know what else would happen?"

"No."

"Anarchy. Imagine a world where everyone could peer into each others' heads, where people could kill you with a touch and no one would be the wiser, where everyone could disappear like your friend Sam. Imagine that world."

I can imagine it. I'm not so certain it would be anarchy like he claims.

"Imagine someone, a homicidal maniac, say, had your gift—could kill with a touch. How would you know they had killed anyone when the cause of death cannot be readily determined?

"No. Our gifts *must* stay controlled, limited, for the benefit of society."

I can see his point. If everyone had our gifts, laws would have to change. The world would become a very different place, potentially a much scarier place.

I still don't feel any effects from the alcohol, but his hand on my shoulder is really bugging me.

"Would you mind if I sat down over there," I say, pointing to one of the chairs. "I need to give my eyes a rest."

"Go right ahead. It's been a long day for you, I know. A lot to take in," he says. "But it's for the best. It truly is."

"Thank you," I say.

"I'm glad to have you with me," he says. At this point, I would expect him to shake my hand, but he doesn't. He's still wary of me.

I head to the chair, ready to take a nap.

CHAPTER 50

I lean back in the chair and close my eyes.

I need to know.

My vision shifts

I'm looking into a room from a doorway. Amy, Tony, and Sam are each strapped into chairs. Their heads are all leaning in different directions. They don't seem coherent. There are no leads to their chests, or anything to monitor them like I had been monitored.

There is a table with three separate series of serum, just like I had seen at the Division Six headquarters. Only, the first two bottles of each series are empty. They've already started.

Three more to go until the binder.

I don't see why these people are so lucky. I've been loyal for years.

Miss Tanaka. I'm in her head again. She's jealous. Maybe I can use that.

I have no idea how.

I wait in her head, watching.

Slowly, the three of them start to come out of it, just like I did. How long did Joe wait? A few minutes between each one?

Miss Tanaka looks down at her watch.

I wonder if Mr. Archon can hear me think while I'm in someone else's head.

I suspect, if he could, he'd be waking me up right now.

Stop thinking. Just wait. Wait for the right time.

I have an inkling of a plan, but I dare not think on it for fear of giving it away. I don't even know how much of it I know. I just hope it comes to me when I need it.

The seconds tick by on her watch.

She looks up.

"How are you all?" he asks.

"Let us go," Sam says.

"You really must stop asking for that," Miss Tanaka says. "I can't let you go now. If I don't finish the treatment, you'll die."

She looks down at her watch again. I want to see their reactions, see Sam's reaction, but I'm stuck in Miss Tanaka's head.

"Time for number three."

First one is for Sam. She wipes Sam's arm with iodine and injects her.

Then Tony.

Then Amy.

And one by one, they start screaming.

I remember the pain, now. I had pushed it from my mind, but I remember and I don't want to watch. But I have to watch, I have to stay. I'll only have a moment in which to act, whatever that action might be, and if I miss it, or if Mr. Archon is peering in on my thoughts right now, then it's all over. I can't let that happen.

While they scream, Miss Tanaka calmly goes through and fills each of the syringes with the fourth dose.

Eventually, the pain subsides and their muscles relax. Their heads begin to hang to the back or to the side as their necks can no longer hold the weight.

And then their eyes flicker open.

Coherent again.

Like I was.

I wonder.

Will Sam be able to see into my mind like I can see into hers? Or will she be different? Will she be like Mr. Archon, who can walk and talk and see in my head and put thoughts in my mind any old time he pleases without any apparent side effects? Or will she have some other new ability that's as different from mine as she is from me?

Miss Tanaka goes through the ritual of complaining to herself and watching her watch.

I can't believe he's making me do this.

She checks her watch.

Why doesn't he want me to have the treatment?

She checks her watch.

I was loyal.

Checks her watch.

It's time.

Again, iodine, injection, pain.

And I'm stuck watching.

One more treatment. After this, she'll give them the binder. I can't let her do that. How do I stop it?

Sam and Amy wake up first. Tony takes a little longer. Now is the time.

I leave Miss Tanaka's head, and I'm back in my own. But I don't wait.

I need to tell you something, Amy. I need to tell you. The world shifts.

I'm looking up at the ceiling. My vision is a little blurry. My body doesn't feel quite right.

God that hurt. I don't know if I can do that again.

Don't speak Amy, it's Steve.

I feel so funny.

Can you hear me, Amy? It's Steve.

I'm going to kick that woman in the crotch when she lets me off this chair.

Amy!

Miss Tanaka is picking up the first syringe. The one for Sam.

Amy! I don't have much time!

I watch it go into Sam's arm. I can feel the terror building in Amy.

Not again. I can't do it again.

I feel the scrapes as she tries to free herself from her bonds. It's not working.

Amy! When you wake up this time, fry the lights! Before she gives you the binder, fry the lights!

Miss Tanaka gives Tony his shot. The screams from Sam are already starting.

Please Amy! Do you hear me? Fry the lights when you wake up!

Miss Tanaka picks up the third syringe and Amy watches it get closer. She watches as it goes in.

Amy! The lights!

And then pain throughout my body.

The world shifts.

And I'm sitting on the chair again, and I haven't got a clue if she heard me.

CHAPTER 51

I hear footsteps.

She didn't hear you, but I did. Nice try, Steve.

I open my eyes.

The footsteps don't belong to Mr. Archon. They belong to one of his henchmen, and the man has his gun drawn and pointed right at me.

"Mr. Archon wants to see you. Get up."

He motions with the gun.

I can't stop a bullet. I probably won't die, but it'll hurt.

I push myself out of the chair, which had been terribly comfortable. I could have slept in it for real.

"Which way?" I ask.

He points to a door at the back of the room.

"That way."

I start walking.

I could take the man's life, and I'm sure Mr. Tanaka knows that. Maybe he even told the guy with the gun. It doesn't matter. I'd have to deal with those memories for a moment, and I'm sure there are others watching. I'd be dead or incapacitated before I had a chance to get to more people. I'm not a mass murder machine.

And there's only one man's life I want to take.

Without him, maybe Joe wouldn't be dead. Maybe Max wouldn't either, and Taggart probably wouldn't be in the situation he's in, either. Maybe Joe could have figured out the treatment anyway, and given it to all of us.

And then what? You'd all live happily ever after? It doesn't work that way, Steve.

Oh? How does it work? We all live like slaves under your rule?

I thought you were going to cooperate.

I try to think of nothing. It's difficult with my rage burning down inside me.

We come to an intersection between hallways, and the gunman tells me to go right. At the end of the hallway, outside a glass door with the Archon Global logo etched into it, he says, "In here."

Through the glass, I see Mr. Archon sitting at his desk. He's staring straight at me. Behind him, windows show a view of the lake, the moonlight glinting like daggers off the ripples in its surface.

I push open the door and the gunman ushers me through.

"You know what I do to traitors?" Mr. Archon asks.

"You kill them," I say.

"Sometimes. Sometimes, I make them watch the person they love suffer. Sometimes I make them give someone else the thing they most want. Whatever hurts more."

"What are you going to do to me?" I ask.

Mr. Archon laughs.

"You think you're a traitor? Think again. I knew you would try something. You had to. You had to push the boundaries. I understand. I mean, you've been on your own for thirty years, ever since you killed your parents. You should be expected to lash out at restrictions."

My parents. He knows about them.

Of course. I told Sam about it while he was in my head.

"Good. You know I was watching. I'm always watching. Joe did his job well. It's a shame he had to turn on me.

"So, here's what you are going to do for me. I know about how you kill people, how you take the things that are most important to them. What secrets do you know, Steve? What little secrets are lodged in your head?"

"I don't have any secrets."

It's a lie. He knows it.

"Oh, but you do. You killed Joe. I know that. There wasn't a mark on his body when we found him. You've got his memories inside your head, and I want them. Every last thing you can dredge up about the formula."

"Why? You already have the formula," I say.

"All but a piece, a piece that Joe kept from everyone. I don't know how he did it, but he did, and I want to know. I need to know. And if you don't, that young woman in there, the one with the scar? The one you tried to contact? She dies."

He's got it... Stop. Don't think about it.

"You can't. You promised..."

"Oh, I know I promised. But you promised, too. So, here's your chance. Show me the memories, show me the missing piece, and all is forgiven."

The memory of the letter comes to the front of my mind, and I can't stop it. It's not what Joe would have wanted.

"See?" Mr. Archon says. "More like that. Although, I am surprised to hear that Joe would want you to destroy his life's work. That truly would be a shame."

"No." I say.

Mr. Archon slaps his hands on the desk and leans forward, stares into my eyes.

"You're willing to let her die?"

"I won't do it. You know those monsters you talked about? The psychopaths that would take their powers and use them to destroy? You're right. That would happen. And you are one of them."

His face turns red, his breath comes hard. I've angered him. I prepare myself to take the brunt of his ire.

"You will show me, now."

The brunt of his ire is not what I expect.

The world shifts.

CHAPTER 52

I see myself fall to the ground on the other side of the desk. The gunman is surprised. His gun goes off, a crack in the air. The window to the lake shatters behind my new body.

I'm in Mr. Archon's head.

Ah, interesting. I hadn't thought you would try this. You can't stay here forever, you know.

I know. But I can stay long enough.

Long enough for what? You can't do anything to me while you're lying on the floor.

Mr. Archon stands and walks over to my body. He kicks it.

And see what I can do to you? I could kill you while you're in my head. I know you come out dizzy. I know what it takes for you to do this. You think you can stop me from doing what I want? You made a mistake, Steve.

"Go kill the girl," Mr. Archon says to his henchman.

"Yes, sir," says the henchman, and he leaves.

Shit.

Yes, Steve. Shit. You still have time to stop it, you know.

Yes. I do. From here.

Though I don't know how.

Mr. Archon laughs. *You are like a child. You went into hiding, never learned a thing about what you can do because it frightened you. Fear is what limits people like you, Steve. Fear of being excellent. Fear of what other people might think.*

I was never afraid. But I was. I was afraid of myself. Afraid of what I did to other people.

Yes. What you didn't realize, Steve, and maybe you will never understand. You, I, we are better than them. We are the pinnacle of our race, now.

You run around, trying to avoid hurting people, but you still hurt them, didn't you.

He kicks my body again.

I want those memories, Steve. We need the final piece of the puzzle. You have about three more seconds before my man puts a half-dozen bullets in your girl's head and ends her life. You don't want that, do you? I can stop it. I can tell him right now to stop.

Sam! The urge to give in so that Sam will live surges through me. I resist. I can prevent more people like him if I keep Joe's secrets to myself. If I die, the secret is gone.

I won't let you die, Steve. Not now, not ever. I'll kill everyone you love, including those humans, Mary and George. I'll keep you in pain so great that you will yield to me eventually. You will want to die, and you'll give up the secret in exchange for me allowing you to die. That is your future, Steve.

Through Mr. Archon's eyes, I can see my body. My hand is so close to his foot. I try to move it. Fail.

See? You can do nothing this way. He's standing over her, now, Steve. I just need one word from you. One simple word. Just say, 'yes,' and she'll live.

The lights go out.

I flee Mr. Archon's head as fast as I can.

Even as the world shifts, I reach out for his leg.

My head swims.

I've got the leg. His sock is between me and my goal.

A force, the only way to describe it, strikes me, tries to pull me away, but I hold on to his leg.

Together, we crash through the glass wall.

The sock comes down a bit.

I reach my other hand out, try to catch his leg above the sock.

He kicks at me with his other foot, smashes me in the nose. It causes me to miss my attempt at his leg. My nose swells. I feel blood rush out. It quickly becomes hard to breathe.

I try again.

Breathing doesn't matter.

I just need...

No Steve!

The blast of his voice in my head hurts.

He can hurt people just by thinking about it.

If he didn't know before, he knows now.

I reach my hand out, above the suck.

My fingertips feel skin.

Another kick from him. His heel crushes my eye, but I don't let go, despite the pain flooding through my head.

Skin.

No!

The flood of his memories, a lifetime of insanity and megalomania flood into me as I take everything he has.

Through his presence in my head, I feel the horror of losing himself, piece by piece, as if time has slowed to a standstill, until the presence pops and disappears.

And in less than a second, he's inside me, and my body starts using his life force to heal my injuries.

I hear a gunshot. Two. Three.

"Sam!"

I want to get up, go to her rescue.

But I can't.

The world spins, even as I lie here on the floor.

I can't breathe.

I can't take the pain.

Not anymore.

CHAPTER 53

Sam.

Her face floats in my memories.

I search back through them for all the good moments, the times we laid together, our bodies naked in the cold of the night, the loneliness of being who we were.

All I have left now are memories.

Each memory, a wound and a balm.

I'll not look them away again.

I didn't kill her.

Didn't I? I could have saved her. I could have told him what he wanted to hear, then kill him.

But I couldn't do that. I couldn't risk telling him and never knowing if I could get close to him again.

The pain is receding. My body working to block it out. I probably won't be able to see out of my left eye for a week, but it will come around.

I've got to get up.

I open my right eye. It's dark in the room, but that's fine. I can still see, even if the moonlight wasn't shining through the empty window.

"Steve?"

It's Sam's voice. A latent memory.

I shake my head.

No, that was a mistake. It's still swimming with dizziness and pain.

I hear footsteps.

I look down the hall.

"Steve!" A shout of worry. Sam's voice.

There are three people walking down the hall. The one in front breaks into a run.

Sam stops in front of me, kneels down.

She's alive, not Memorex.

There's a bullet hole in her neck, but it's healing. It'll take longer than my wounds, since she can't steal someone's life force like I can, but she'll live. It wasn't in her head.

"You're alive," I say.

"You look like hell," she says.

"I thought..."

She doesn't need to read my mind to know what I was going to say.

"Amy put out the lights, caused an overload. That asshole comes in, starts shooting at me, but that serum, it did things to us. I threw him against the wall with my mind. And then Tony broke free and broke his neck."

"Good," I say.

I blink my right eye, trying to clear the fuzziness.

"Looks like you got Mr. Archon," Sam says.

"I did. What about Miss Tanaka?"

"Took a bullet from the gunman. She won't live."

"The other guards?"

"They came running with the gunshots. Tony took care of them."

I reach up with my hand, touch her face.

"He tried to use you to make me give up the formula. He said he would kill you if I didn't. I was going to let you die."

The admission makes me feel better, though I fear her reaction. I don't want her upset with me.

She leans down and kisses me. My lips tingle when they meet hers.

When she pulls away, she says, "I would have died to keep it away from him. What his company did to us, to our friends... You did the right thing."

Did I? I don't know.

"He threatened Mary and George, too."

"He's dead now, though. You won."

Wait. Mary... George... Taggart.

"Do we know where the rest of the treatments are?"

"Not yet, but we haven't started searching."

I close my eyes. I don't want to delve into Mr. Archon's memories just yet, but I don't have a choice. Taggart's life depends on it.

I just need to find...

Got it.

"Help me up," I say.

Sam does.

When I'm standing, I notice Amy.

And I realize, she's been there the whole time, and I haven't been affected by her pheromones.

"You heard me," I say to her.

"I thought it was a dream," she says. "But the idea sounded good, so I did it."

But she did hear me, and that's enough. I can do what Brad Archon could do. Perhaps not as well, but that doesn't matter.

The dizziness is finally starting to fade.

"I know where the treatments are," I say. "If we hurry..."

"There's not enough time," Sam says, sounding defeated. "It's a two hour drive."

I look down at Brad Archon, ex-CEO of Archon Global.

"I beat him once," I say. "I'm tired of your friends dying."

She looks at me and smiles.

"So am I."

CHAPTER 54

Just outside the gate to the canyon that leads to Brad Archon's compound, a car waits. It's black, and looks very much like a Division Six car.

As Sam drives her van through the gate, the car flashes its lights at us, then pulls out to block the road.

Sam brings the van to a stop.

A woman gets out of the passenger side door.

It's Mary.

"We've got Taggart," she says.

I don't know what I'll do with Joe's knowledge. It will stay with me as long as I live.

But I know exactly what we're going to do with one batch of the remaining serum.

"Let's get him in the van," I say. "Let's give Taggart his freedom."

About The Author

Mark Fassett lives in western Washington with his wife, children, and cats. He's a fantasy and science fiction author whose novels include *Shattered*, *Fragments*, and *Questioner's Shadow*. He's also written several novellas in those same genres. In the past, he had extensive experience in the mobile game business and was involved with some of the top selling titles at the time of their release, including multiple *Duke Nukem Mobile* games and *Guitar Hero World Tour Mobile*.

Learn About New Releases

Visit http://markfassett.com/newsletter to join my mailing list and get notified about my newest releases!

Find Me Online

Blog — http://www.markfassett.com
Twitter — http://twitter.com/mark_fassett
Facebook — http://www.facebook.com/markfassett.writer
E-Mail — mark@markfassett.com